A pyramid rising from the... A mysterious talisman with the power to command the elements…

An occult riddle concealing the secret of immortality…

And a diabolical enemy bent on destroying anyone who seeks it.

A deadly showdown at the end of the world is just the opening move in Dane Maddock's war with the shadowy Prometheus group. Joined by archaeologists Jade Ihara and Nick Kismet, Prometheus' sworn enemy, Maddock and Bones make a perilous descent into the world of the arcane. Who will win the race to possess the ultimate power?

Praise for David Wood and Sean Ellis!

"Dane and Bones. Together they're unstoppable. Rip roaring action from start to finish. Wit and humor throughout. Just one question - how soon until the next one? Because I can't wait."

-Graham Brown, author of Shadows of the Midnight Sun

"What an adventure! A great read that provides lots of action, and thoughtful insight as well, into strange realms that are sometimes best left unexplored." -Paul Kemprecos, author of Cool Blue Tomb and the NUMA Files

ARCANUM

A DANE MADDOCK ADVENTURE

DAVID WOOD
SEAN ELLIS

ARCANUM
Copyright 2018 by David Wood

Published by Adrenaline Press
www.adrenaline.press

Adrenaline Press is an imprint of Gryphonwood Press
www.gryphonwoodpress.com

ISBN-13: 978-1-940095-92-9
ISBN-10: 1-940095-92-1

BOOKS and SERIES by DAVID WOOD

The Dane Maddock Adventures
Dourado
Cibola
Quest
Icefall
Buccaneer
Atlantis
Ark
Xibalba
Loch
Solomon Key

Dane and Bones Origins
Freedom
Hell Ship
Splashdown
Dead Ice
Liberty
Electra
Amber
Justice
Treasure of the Dead

Adventures from the Dane Maddock Universe
Destination-Rio
Destination-Luxor
Berserk
The Tomb
Devil's Face
Outpost

Arcanum
Magus
Brainwash
Herald
Maug
Cavern

Jade Ihara Adventures (with Sean Ellis)
Oracle
Changeling
Exile

Bones Bonebrake Adventures
Primitive
The Book of Bones
Skin and Bones
Venom

Jake Crowley Adventures (with Alan Baxter)
Blood Codex
Anubis Key

Brock Stone Adventures
Arena of Souls
Track of the Beast (forthcoming)

Myrmidon Files (with Sean Ellis)
Destiny
Mystic

Sam Aston Investigations (with Alan Baxter)
Primordial
Overlord

PROLOGUE

Plymouth, England 1910

The coachwork canopy of the Lanchester 16 kept the persistent drizzle at bay, but did little to banish the chill. The driver seemed impervious to both, but the young boy who sat beside him had lived most of his life in the desert and the cool, damp air cut deep into him despite his best efforts to disappear completely into a heavy wool blanket.

The boy's name was Hassan ibn Ali, though he had not been called this in many years. His master—the man who now drove the Lanchester along the muddy old carriage road—called him 'Blue Boy' or sometimes just 'Blue,' and mostly that was how he thought of himself. The master was not a cruel man, though Blue greatly feared to cause him displeasure. He had seen the man call down lightning from the heavens and that alone was enough to terrify him. Besides, he liked the color, especially the cerulean hue of a cloudless sky at noon. Whenever he saw that, which wasn't often at this latitude, he thought of home and the life he had lived before the master's arrival.

It almost felt like a dream to him now.

Their destination was a great stone house, perched atop a hill. Blue supposed that on a clear day, the house would have a spectacular view of Plymouth Sound to the east but on this dreary night, the only indication that they were near water was the relentless pulses of illumination against the dismal clouds. Two flashes every ten seconds from the Eddystone lighthouse which lay several miles offshore, at the entrance to the harbor.

The house was dark and looked deserted, but as they rolled up the drive toward it, the driver worked the klaxon, sending out a piercing note to herald their arrival. As the car pulled to a stop, a door opened revealing lamplight within. The Lanchester's engine coughed and sputtered for several seconds and then with one final harsh bang, like a gunshot, fell silent. Blue shed the blanket like the second skin it had become and with great reluctance opened the door and stepped out into the gray drizzle. As soon as he was in the open, he deployed a large umbrella and immediately found some shelter under its capacious dome, but he knew this would only be a brief reprieve. He circled around to the opposite side of the automobile and held the umbrella high above the door to protect the driver as he emerged. As the umbrella moved away from Blue, he again felt the chilly rain on the back of his neck but he endured this discomfort with gritted teeth. His duties did not require him to be warm or dry.

He had to hurry to keep up with the master's long determined strides, which posed a new set of problems. The mud was slippery underfoot and with his arm extended, it took all his concentration to keep his footing. By some miracle, they reached the front door where a man holding an oil lamp gestured for them to hurry inside.

The old house was draughty and Blue could hear the sound of water trickling against stone, indicating at least one leak in the old thatch, but it was a marginal improvement. He shook the water off the umbrella before setting it aside, and then helped the master out of his cloak and galoshes. Beneath his wet weather clothes, the master wore a long saffron colored gown, decorated with spangles, and wound about his head was a white turban, adorned with a star ruby cabochon brooch. The costume was probably meant to make him look like a holy man or mystic from the Far East, but the overall effect was a touch too theatrical, making him seem more like a stage magician or worse, a carnival mountebank.

It was a deliberate choice, more effective at altering his appearance and hiding his true identity than any magic spell.

He did not always dress like this. Only when he was with Blue… Only when he was Adam Garral. And when he was Garral, he wanted those who saw him to remember his outlandish attire, not his true face.

The man with the lamp did not speak, and with the light held before him, his face remained hidden in shadow. When they had doffed their wet weather clothes, the man turned and beckoned them to follow.

They were led to an interior room where a roaring fire at last drove the chill from Blue's bones.

He unconsciously moved closer to the hearth, savoring the warmth that radiated from it. The man with the lamp—Blue now saw that he was about the same age as the master, of similar build and handsome, though heavier—set the light down on a table, and settled himself into one of the chairs arrayed around it.

Garral glanced down at the seated man for a moment. "Still playing at cards, Alick?"

Blue craned his head to get a better look and saw dozens of rectangular pieces of pasteboard spread out on the tabletop. He edged closer, curious despite his desire to stay near the fire, and saw familiar symbols sketched on some of the cards— swords, cups, pentacles—and crudely drawn figures on others. Most were blank.

The man at the table looked up, a scowl on his slightly plump face. "I hate that name."

"I know," Garral said, gravely, then burst out laughing.

The other man shook his head irritably. "Why are you here, Adam?"

"You know why," Garral replied. "The mirror. You have it. I want to look into it."

"The mirror is a bauble. A parlor game."

"Then you should have no objection to letting me have a look."

The card maker regarded him with naked suspicion. "You've learned something, haven't you? Some new insight?"

"I won't know until I've tried."

The card maker nodded slowly. "Very well, but you must share it with me."

Garral inclined his head in a gesture of surrender.

The other man leaned to the side and began rooting in a carpet bag that rested alongside his chair. When he straightened, he held in his hands something that looked to Blue like a misshapen dinner plate made of smoky glass. He placed it on the tabletop and slid it toward the visitor.

Garral sucked in his breath when he saw it but tried to hide his reaction behind another smile. He stared down at the obsidian disc for a moment, his expression only mildly curious, but Blue could sense the eagerness in him. Garral's entire body seemed to vibrate with it, like a plucked harp string. Blue took an involuntary step closer, as if drawn by his master's magnetism.

Garral abruptly pivoted, grabbed a chair and adjusted it so that it was positioned in front of the black mirror, and then, snapping the sleeves of his ornate gown with a dramatic flourish, lowered himself into it.

He placed his hands on the table, palms down to either side of the mirror, and closed his eyes as if meditating. After a few seconds, his eyelids fluttered open and he reached up with this right hand to touch the ruby on his turban with a finger. His lips began moving, framing a silent incantation. Blue knew this was a pretense, a charade to divert their host's attention away from what Garral was doing with his left hand. Under the table, hidden from the other man's view, but not from Blue, Garral was gripping a small block of cobalt colored stone.

The object was a talisman of some sort. Blue still remembered the first time he had seen it, the night Garral had called down fire from the sky, the same night that he had entered into his master's service. The stone, unlike the ruby brooch, was a source of real power, though Garral had never succeeded in duplicating what had happened on that fateful night. Now, or so it seemed, he was trying to unlock its potential in a different way.

Garral now leaned over the flat black mirror as if to stare into it, and slowly, tentatively, reached down to touch it with his right hand.

The moment his fingers made contact, he jerked them back as if the mere touch had burned him. Blue ran to his master's side, reflexively laying a steadying hand on Garral's shoulder. In that same instant, Garral touched the mirror again.

A memory sprang unbidden into Blue's mind. He vividly recalled the first time he had seen the mirror, resting on an altar in a room made of jade, hidden at the heart of a dark pyramid temple in the jungles of New Spain—the land now known as Mexico.

But no, that couldn't be right. He had never seen this strange mirror before… Had not felt even a faint glimmer of recognition upon seeing it.

Yet his memory of its discovery was beyond vivid.

A score of men had died on the journey to reach the temple, felled by wild beasts and fever, hazards common to the emerald hell through which they had blazed a path, seeking gold and other riches. Five more had died inside the maze of passages that cut through the pyramids interior, and what had killed them was beyond Blue's comprehension. Everything about the pyramid defied reason. The walls were joined at impossible angles, like something that could only exist in a nightmare....

He remembered taking it from the altar... Picking it up with his own hands....

Now he remembered another day, many months later. He was on a ship... Not a steam-powered vessel, but a sailing ship, a massive craft with three masts stabbing up into a cloudless azure sky. The riggings hung empty, the sails lowered, the ship unmoving. The crew, swarthy, rough looking men, stood in rows on the deck, similarly motionless. A second ship lay alongside the first, the two held together with ropes and grappling hooks. Men, armed with long knives and old matchlock pistols and muskets, were crossing over.

Pirates, Blue thought, and then a name came to mind.

Drake.

Blue staggered back a step, and as he lost contact with Garral, the flood of memories ceased with the abruptness of a door slamming shut. He shook off a sudden sensation of vertigo and returned his attention to Garral, desperate to know what he had just experienced, but afraid to ask.

Garral had not moved. He sat as still as a statue, one hand touching the obsidian mirror, the other surreptitiously gripping the lapis lazuli talisman. Blue started to reach for him again, but hesitated, remembering that they were not alone.

The card maker was staring intently, almost hungrily, at Garral.

Before Blue could do anything else, Garral jerked in his chair and then sat up straight. His head turned back and forth, eyes dancing as if trying to remember where he was.

"Adam," the awed card maker whispered. "What did you see?"

Garral stared at him mutely for a moment, then reached out across the table with both hands. His left seized one of the blank paste board cards. His right wrapped around the long shaft of a pencil. He brought both to him and then began sketching an image.

The tip of the pencil moved with preternatural swiftness and precision, and in mere seconds, an image took shape. It was a human form, and for a moment, Blue thought he was looking at the likeness of the crucified Christ. Garral continued sketching, adding details—small figures surrounding the central figure, a web of lines that reminded Blue of the riggings on the sailing vessel he had… remembered? Imagined?

Garral stopped sketching, contemplating the

sketch for a moment, and then laid the pencil down beside the card.

"That?" The card maker said. "That is what you saw? What is it?"

Garral returned a cryptic smile. "Why, my dear Alick, it's everything."

McMurdo Station, Antarctica—Now

"When I got on this plane, I really thought it meant I was done freezing my balls off." Uriah "Bones" Bonebrake gazed down the lowering ramp of the US Air Force C-17A Globemaster III extended range cargo plane and out across the stark white Antarctic landscape and shook his head sadly.

"You know what happens when you assume."

Bones turned and met the smirking gaze of his tormentor. "Yes Jade, I do. I know that some *ass—you*—will give *me* a freaking spelling lesson."

"I don't often take the big guy's side," said Dane Maddock, standing right behind Bones and next to Jade. "But he's right."

Jade Ihara rolled her eyes. "You always take his side, Maddock. That's your biggest problem."

"That's because he's figured out that I'm usually right," Bones said, with a grin that was more menacing than friendly. "And you haven't. That's *your* biggest problem. As rescues go, this one kind of blows. We're still in Antarctica, we still have that orb we picked up at the Outpost, and as far as we know, this Prometheus group—whoever they really are—is still after us. And I'm still freezing my balls off. Which part of that did I get wrong, Jade?"

"The part where you actually have balls, I think."

"Play nice kids," Maddock said. "Let's not fight in front of our new friends."

"Sorry," said Rose Greer, standing just behind him. "But I'm with Bones. It's been fun, but I am so over this place."

Maddock blew out his breath in a long audible sigh. He could see the exhalation floating in front of him, a vapor cloud turning into ice crystals before his very eyes. "Well, we can't leave until we return the snowcat."

"I hate to be the bearer of bad news, but I think that ship has sailed." This came from the remaining member of their group, Nick Kismet. "We may still be in Antarctica, but we're about two thousand miles from your snowcat. I don't think I'm going to be able to convince the pilot to make another trip like that anytime soon. Especially not with what happened this time out."

Five hours earlier, Kismet and Jade had swooped in with the C-17 to pluck the rest of them from the middle of a harrowing firefight on the polar ice. The snowcat in question—a loaner—had carried Maddock, Bones and Rose from Novo Base on the part of the continent that was closest to the southern tip of Africa, to the Mühlig-Hofmann

Mountains where they had discovered what appeared to be a man-made pyramid, jutting up from the ice like an enormous black tooth. Stranger still, they had discovered a tunnel in the ice which took them inside the structure, where they had found a strange spherical artifact with extraordinary, and quite possibly supernatural properties. Shortly after finding it however, they had been attacked by a group of gunmen—agents of a mysterious group that Nick Kismet had subsequently identified as *Prometheus.*

Although they had made it out of the pyramid with the artifact, they had been outnumbered and outgunned, and the situation had looked pretty dire until the unexpected arrival of Kismet and Jade aboard the C-17. Unfortunately, they had been obliged to leave the snowcat behind. If the surviving Prometheus gunmen hadn't already helped themselves to the tracked all-terrain vehicle, it would eventually be covered over by an ever-deepening blanket of ice and swept away by the relentlessly advancing glacier.

After the rescue, the plane had flown nonstop over the frozen continent to McMurdo Station on the Ross Ice shelf, and as Kismet had pointed out, despite the fact that they were still on the same continent, the snowcat was as far away from them now as Los Angeles was from Detroit, and every inch of it was in the harshest, most unforgiving landscape on earth.

"Screw the pilots," Bones said. "You couldn't convince *me* to go back. Not for a million bucks."

Maddock wondered if a million dollars would cover the replacement cost of the snowcat and sighed again. It would be a hell of a tax write-off, at least.

The cargo ramp settled into place and with one final whine of effort, the hydraulic actuators went silent. Beyond the ramp lay the packed snow of Williams Field—one of the official runways servicing McMurdo Station.

"Actually," Bones said as he stared out at the brutally austere environment, "I'm not even sure I want to get off this plane. Can't we just hang here while they top off the tanks?"

Kismet shook his head. "I'm afraid this bird won't be heading back to civilization until we've accomplished our primary mission."

"Believe it or not," Jade chimed in, with more than a hint of sarcasm in her tone, "We didn't actually come down here just to pull your asses out of the fire."

"Oh, if only there had been a fire," Bones sighed.

"Come on, Jade." Maddock said. "Don't tell me you just happened to be in the neighborhood. You knew right where to find us. And you already said that Tam sent you here. So what's really going on?"

Jade glanced over at Kismet. "Do you want to tell them, or should I?"

Kismet shrugged. "They're your friends."

"I wouldn't go that far," Bones grumbled.

"Me either," Jade shot back acidly, but then she shifted her gaze to Maddock and her expression softened a little. She pointed out at an approaching red shape, a massive vehicle trailing a cloud of blowing snow. "There's Ivan. Come on. I'll tell you what I know on the way, and Nick can fill in the gaps."

With that, she moved past Bones and started down the ramp. Maddock knew she was being stingy with the information just to piss him off. Evidently, she was still sore about how their relationship had ended. He also knew the only way he was going to get any answers was to play along, so he followed her down to the ice.

Bones just shook his head. "Now I gotta ride with some dude named Ivan. I'll bet he smells like beets. This day just keeps getting better."

PART ONE—JADE

1

Peru—one week earlier

You really should consider carrying a pistol."

Jade Ihara glanced over at the lanky, sandy-haired man who had just growled at her, and frowned. "That's what I have you for," she retorted.

Pete "Professor" Chapman shook his head wearily. "I'm not Rambo. Even I need back-up once in a while."

Jade didn't have any real objection to guns, and had used them once or twice in particularly sticky situations—situations a lot like this, actually—but there were some very good reasons why she chose not to make a habit of carrying, not the least of which was that most of the countries where she operated—Jade was an archaeologist specializing in pre-Columbian American cultures—took a dim view of visiting scholarly types walking around packing heat. It was true; Professor wasn't Rambo, and she wasn't Indy-anna Jones or Angelina what's-her-name… The *Tomb Raider* chick. Actually, if anyone was Indiana Jones, it was Professor in his Explorer fedora, a lucky charm he'd picked up in Costa Rica during one of their adventures together. But headgear or no, running around the jungle, looting temples and blasting away the bad guys wasn't her standard operating procedure.

"In case you haven't no—"

She broke off as another volley of automatic rifle fire tore into the sandstone right above her head, spraying them with chips of stone and hot lead fragments. The gunmen were shooting from multiple locations, closing in on them like a noose.

Jade ducked reflexively, even though she was already ducking just about as low as was humanly possible. Professor calmly stabbed his semi-automatic pistol in the direction from which the fire had come, squeezed off several shots in rapid succession.

Professor was actually a lot more Rambo-like than he cared to admit. Despite his nickname, he wasn't really a college teacher—not at the moment, anyway—and hadn't been when he'd earned the nickname early on in his first career as a Navy SEAL. His teammates had started calling him that because of his encyclopedic knowledge of just about any subject imaginable and because of his tendency to lecture. He was currently working for a highly-classified elite US government task force called the 'Myrmidons' and more specifically, acting as Jade's bodyguard-slash-assistant, which was why *he* had no compunction about carrying unregistered weapons wherever Jade's work took her. In truth, Jade wasn't even sure how he was able to smuggle the weapons into the various destinations they visited, but she trusted that he would always be ready to face down whatever threat presented itself.

Sometimes—this time, in fact—the threat was

more than he could reasonably handle, but Jade really didn't see how the situation would be that much different if she was armed, too.

"I'll think about it," she said, but before she could say any more on the topic, Professor grabbed her arm and dragged her away from the sloping stone face, and toward the nearly impenetrable jungle. A hail of bullets tore into the rock wall, right where she had been crouching a moment before.

Another burst from a rifle raked the jungle canopy as the two of them plunged headlong into the underbrush. Roots and vines snagged Jade's feet and would have tripped her up, but the tangle of ferns and thorny branches kept her upright, even as they lashed her face and arms. Professor had traded his pistol for a machete, but with the gunmen behind them, there wasn't time to do much more than swing wildly and hope for the best. There was a perfectly good trail, not fifty yards away, but Jade knew they'd never reach it, and even if they did, it would only make it easier for the gunmen to find them.

After just a few seconds of crashing through the brush, Professor seemed to get the hang of moving through the dense rainforest, finding the path of least resistance, but Jade could hear shouts and movement in the jungle all around them. The gunmen were still close, and probably closing in.

"This way," Professor whispered, pulling her along as he ducked through a gap in the thicket that looked barely wide enough for a cat to slip through.

Jade did her best to move stealthily, but the rustling noise she made as she pushed forward sounded to her like a jet taking off. Something snagged her hair and jerked her head back. Just a branch, but it was enough to stop her in her tracks. She wrapped a hand around her ponytail, gripping it like she would a length of rope to keep her hair from being torn out by the roots, and then drove forward again, hastening after Professor.

The site they were visiting, located in the remote jungles of Manu National Park, a biosphere reserve with few roads and only a handful of permanent occupants—all indigenous natives from the friendly Matsigenga tribe—was supposed to be safe; safe of course being a relative term in the jungle.

They had come here to investigate the so-called "pyramids" of Paratoari, a series of sandstone formations in the Peruvian jungle, first noticed in satellite photographs taken in 1976. Seen from space, the formations—at least eight uniformly shaped and sized objects arranged in evenly-spaced parallel rows—appeared too symmetrical to be the work of geological forces, and for at least twenty years thereafter, they were believed to be evidence of an undiscovered archaeological site, perhaps even the lost Incan city of Paititi. The first on-site investigation in 1996 however not only confirmed the alternative and boringly-plausible hypothesis that the so-called structures were in fact naturally occurring rock formations but also revealed that they were not as perfectly symmetrical as they appeared in the satellite photographs. This revelation however had not dampened the enthusiasm of fringe archaeology enthusiasts—the sort of people who believed that ancient civilizations were influenced by extraterrestrial visitors.

While Jade did not doubt the accepted truth—that the "pyramids" were just truncated ridge spurs—there was some evidence of an Inca presence in the area, including ancient paved roads, platforms, and petroglyphs, all of which raised the possibility that the Inca might have revered the naturally occurring pyramid-shaped rocks, possibly even excavating passages and interior chambers in which to hide the long-sought legendary gold of Paititi, passages which had subsequently been hidden by the dense jungle foliage. If Paititi did exist, and there were several compelling lines of evidence to suggest that it did, it was almost certainly located somewhere in the region, so why not under the "pyramids"?

It was a longshot of course, but the only way to rule it out definitively was with an on-site survey, which was why Jade and Professor had flown to Cuzco, high in the Andes mountains, and then driven a rented Land Rover down the treacherous and winding primitive roads into the Amazon Basin to a spot near the native settlement of Shintuya on the banks of the Madre de Dios River. The Paratoari site was just a few miles to the west, but getting to it required crossing the river and then bushwhacking through the dense forest. After an hour or so of hacking a path through the foliage, they had stumbled onto what they assumed was a trail cut by some previous expedition. It was only when they neared the pyramid-shaped rocks that they realized who was actually using the trail.

Jade was both physically and mentally prepared—as prepared as anyone could ever really be—for the ordinary dangers common to tropical rain forest ecosystems: animal predators, snakes, spiders and other bugs, toxic plants, mosquito- and water-borne diseases. But she had not anticipated stumbling across a camp of armed men living in the woods.

They were probably drug smugglers, shuttling cocaine from a processing plant hidden in the jungle to an illegal airfield for transport out of the country, or possibly anti-government Shining Path guerillas—or more likely some combination of the two. There weren't supposed to be any drug smugglers or guerillas in the area, but then those people didn't exactly advertise their presence in Trip Advisor.

Bottom line, there were a lot of bad guys, maybe as many as a dozen, and one more pistol between herself and Professor wasn't likely to tip the odds.

2

The green hell seemed to go on forever, but no matter how long they toiled, their pursuers were always close, never more than a few hundred yards away. The gunmen clearly didn't want word of their illicit presence to reach the authorities, and weren't likely to settle for anything less than two bullet-riddled corpses.

They were moving down a gentle slope, which was good, but the area was thick with underbrush and they had to fight for every inch. Then, without any warning, the jungle opened up, like the sea parting in some kind of Biblical miracle. Jade heard Professor shout something—a warning—but before she could fully process the significance of anything she was seeing or hearing, the ground beneath her was abruptly no longer beneath her. She pitched forward, half-sliding, half-falling down a steep embankment toward the muddy water of the Rio Madre de Dios. She barely had time to draw a breath before plunging face first into the surprisingly chilly water.

She thrashed for a moment before righting herself, and as she rubbed the water from her eyes, she could feel the current dragging her along.

"Swim for it!"

Jade craned her head around and found Professor, just a few yards further upriver, swimming with powerful strokes toward the far shore. She also spotted their Rover, a distant speck on the road just above the opposite river bank, falling further away with each passing second, and realized that she needed to be doing the same. She reached out and began clawing and kicking through the water.

Several sharp reports sounded behind her and she heard the harsh crack of bullets splitting the air above her head, sizzling into the water all around. Jade ducked under the surface, both to conceal herself from the shooters and to use the water itself as a shield. High-velocity rounds, like the kind fired by the assault rifles the gunmen were using, shattered on impact with water.

She had seen it on *Mythbusters*, so it had to be true.

She swam underwater for several strokes, feeling much more in her element here than she had in the jungle, but after several seconds, the need to breathe forced her back to the surface. She raised her head cautiously, and saw that she was now a good hundred yards further downriver and more than halfway across. She could see the gunmen behind her, semi-distinct shapes against the verdant backdrop. They had stopped shooting. Jade guessed they had lost track of her, and knew that could change at any second, so she ducked under the surface again and kept swimming until her knees began dragging against the mud in the shallows at the far river bank.

She crawled up onto shore, staying low and moving slow, like a crocodile—

Are there crocodiles here?

The thought triggered a momentary panic. No, there weren't crocodiles, but there were caimans—a smaller but no less dangerous reptilian predator—as well as snakes—and not just any snakes, but anacondas, the largest snakes on earth, some big enough to swallow a human child whole. Ravenous piranhas weren't outside the realm of possibility either, but even deadlier were the threats too small to be seen with the naked eye; insidious flesh- and brain-eating protozoans and parasites.

"Jade!" Professor's hissing voice brought her back to the moment. She turned to look for him, but saw only mud and reeds.

"Where are you?"

Something moved just a few yards away and she nearly screamed before realizing that the mud-covered creature coming toward her *was* Professor.

Totally Rambo, Jade thought.

"These guys can't shoot for crap," he whispered. "But we're not out of their range yet, so stay low until you're on solid ground. Then, when I give the signal, run like hell for the Rover."

Crawling through the mud and running like hell didn't sound like much fun to Jade, but the prospect of a quick motorized escape at the end was more than worth it. "Gotcha," she replied.

"Then move."

Jade started forward, trying to move slow and stealthy, but almost immediately sank up to her elbows in the thick mud.

"Crap," she muttered. She tried to extricate herself, fighting the muck for every inch.

"Now," Professor shouted. "Run for it!"

"Really?"

She gave up on slow and stealthy, and wrenched herself out of the mud, thrashing and stumbling forward. Professor was twenty yards ahead of her sprinting through the grass, practically floating over the mud flats.

The familiar crack of gunfire sounded again. Jade glanced back. She couldn't make out the gunmen on the bank, but she did spot three… No, four shapes splashing in the water, halfway across the river.

Jeez, these guys are persistent, she thought.

A bullet creased the air just a few feet to her right, smacking into the mud with an audible hiss. That was all the motivation Jade needed. She launched herself forward, clawing at the mud until, mercifully, she felt something almost like solid ground underfoot.

Professor was now more than fifty yards ahead of her; halfway to the road and the waiting Rover. With his head start, he would at least be able to get the vehicle started so they could take off as soon as she reached it.

Almost unconsciously, she patted her pockets,

checking to make sure that she didn't have the keys.

That would suck.

But no, the keys weren't in her pockets. Professor had driven last, so he almost certainly had the keys.

Unless he lost them while crawling around in the mud. That would really suck.

Suddenly, a thunderous cracking sound filled the air. The noise hit Jade like a slap. She had no idea what had caused it but knew it couldn't be anything good, so she threw herself flat on the ground in a reflex of self-preservation. In the corner of her eye, she saw a bright pink-orange flame, like a signal flare but much faster, streaking over the tall grass at the river's edge, streaking toward the—

There was another loud crack, harsher than a rifle report or even a peal of thunder, and a flash as the Rover transformed into a pillar of smoke and fire.

3

Jade rolled into a protective fetal curl, covering her head with her arms as the hot shock wave slammed into her, and stayed in that position for several seconds afterward as pieces of flaming debris began raining down all around her. By some miracle, none of it found her, but this was little comfort. Without the Rover....

She pushed the dire thought away and raised her head. "Professor? You still with me?"

"Jade! Over here!"

She started to rise, cocking her head to home in on his voice, but he stopped her with a hiss. "Stay down."

Something rustled in the grass beside her and she flinched, half-expecting to find herself staring down the gullet of a black caiman, but it was just Professor. "Stay down," he repeated. "If they suspect we're still alive, they might shoot another RPG."

"What, because blowing up the Rover twice sends a stronger message?"

"I meant shoot it at us. RPGs aren't exactly the ideal antipersonnel weapon, but just like horseshoes, sometimes close is good enough."

"Oh. I knew that."

He looked away, searching the surrounding area as if looking for a target. Jade realized that he had his pistol out.

"I saw three or four of them swimming across,"

she said.

"I know," he said without turning to her.

"Have you got a plan?"

"This is it." He thumbed a lever on the side of his pistol, caught the magazine as it fell from the grip. After a quick visual inspection, he shook his head and slid it home again. "We play possum and hope they don't trip over us."

"How are we going to—"

"Shhh!"

Jade frowned. Was Professor silencing her because the bad guys were close or was he just trying to avoid answering her questions? She wasn't sure which explanation was better, but nevertheless did as instructed, clamping her mouth shut.

At first, the only thing she could hear was the sound of her own breathing, but after a few seconds, she could hear other sounds. The crackling of the flames that were still burning in the wreckage of their Land Rover. The soft rushing sound of the river. The rustling of something or someone moving through the vegetation… Men shouting in Spanish. Not too close, but definitely too close for comfort.

And then she heard something else. The distinctive roar of a jet engine, growing louder with each passing second.

Crap! Just when I thought this day couldn't get any worse.

She jolted as several rapid-fire reports sounded

nearby. Without offering a word of explanation, Professor abruptly rolled over onto her, covering her body with his own, one hand clamped over her mouth. She knew he was just trying to protect her, but it took every ounce of self-control she possessed to simply lay there and let it happen.

A moment later, she heard a scream, which was abruptly cut off by what sounded like a stampede in the tall grass. It took another second or two for the buzz saw report of the distant machine gun to reach her ears, but when it did, she put two and two together.

The approaching aircraft—a helicopter—was shooting at the men on the ground with a large caliber automatic weapon. The kind of weapon soldiers might have.

"We're saved!" she shouted, or tried to. The exclamation was almost completely muffled by Professor's hand, and what came out sounded more like "Wuh say."

"Shhh," he said again, whispering into her ear. "We don't know who that is or what they want. They'll probably shoot first and ask questions later."

She hated to admit it, but he was right. Nobody knew they were out here, which meant the helicopter wasn't there to save them. Even if it was the Peruvian military, ready to take down the smugglers or terrorist or whatever they were, they wouldn't be able to differentiate good guys from bad, not from the air at least.

Okay, so maybe we're not saved.

The noise grew louder, the helicopter beating the air and flattening the grass with its rotor wash, as it descended, setting down on the road near the burning Rover, less than a hundred yards away. There hadn't been any shooting after the initial burst, but all that meant was that the soldiers were waiting for some fool to poke his or her head up so they could shoot it off.

She heard more shouting now, which seemed unusual given the amount of ambient noise. Even more surprising however, was *what* the man was shouting.

"Jade! Jade Ihara!"

"Wuh thu feh?" Jade muttered into Professor's hand.

As if waiting for that cue, he let go, rolling off her. "Someone here to see you," he whispered.

Jade glared at him. "What am I supposed to do?"

Professor shrugged. "Ask them what they want."

"And what if what they want is to blow my head off?"

"I don't think it is, but I'll cover you. Trust me."

"Trust you," she grumbled, but then rose up on all fours and slowly... very slowly, stood with both hands raised high in the air.

As her head came up above the surrounding foliage, she saw clearly the helicopter idling on the ground, a stone's throw from the blasted remains of the Land Rover. It was definitely a military aircraft. Its bulbous fuselage bristling with weapons and rocket pods looked like a gigantic high-tech killer wasp. Half-a-dozen men, all wearing green-gray camouflage uniforms were fanning out from it in a loose semi-circle, and as Jade appeared before them, they all shifted their assault rifles toward her.

"Don't shoot!" she cried. "It's me. I'm Jade."

She didn't know if they could hear or understand, so she reached her hands a little bit higher, and as she did, she realized that one of the men didn't look like the others. Instead of a camouflage uniform and combat gear, he wore denim jeans and a khaki bush shirt, its long sleeves rolled up above his elbows. He had a thick beard and his uncovered head was an unruly black mop, tousled by the persistent rotor wash. He was good-looking, too; not movie-star or male-model pretty-boy handsome, but rougher, more masculine. His dark eyes locked onto her, and as he started toward her, she knew that he was the one who had been calling her name. The man turned away for a moment, shouting to the nearest soldier, who in turn barked an order to the others, and just like that, the rifles were aimed elsewhere.

Okay, that's a hopeful sign, Jade thought.

The man returned his attention to her and kept moving forward until he was only a couple steps away. He cupped a hand over his mouth and in a voice that was only slightly softer than a shout, said, "Dr. Ihara, I presume?"

She grinned, strangely giddy at his use of her academic title. "That's me."

"You can put your hands down," he said, extending his own right hand.

She dropped her arms, feeling a flush of embarrassment, and quickly accepted his hand clasp. "Hi. Call me Jade."

"Nick Kismet."

Kismet? Seriously? What is this guy, a rock star or something? She decided not to say it aloud.

His gaze flitted past her just for a moment, then he added, "Tell your friend that it's safe to come out. We're the good guys."

Jade laughed nervously, then turned, searching the grass for Professor but he was nowhere to be seen. She shrugged. "He's kind of shy. I guess he'll join us when he's ready. So what are you doing here, Nick Kismet?"

"Believe it or not, I was looking for you."

"Well, here I am. But that doesn't really answer my question."

He chuckled softly. "It looks like you guys could use a ride out of here. How about we talk about it on the way?"

"On the way to where?"

His expression became a little more serious. "That's one of the things we need to talk about."

4

After climbing aboard the helicopter, Jade donned a set of earmuff style headphones that, thankfully, brought the noise level from the engines down to a dull roar. After making a futile effort to wipe some of the mud from his fedora, Professor climbed in and took the air chair next to her. The misshapen hat lay on his lap, looking miserable but not defeated. Kismet sat across the aisle, and as both men fitted their commo headsets in place, the rest of the soldiers crowded in, filling up all the other seats and whatever other space they could find. When the last man was in, the aircraft began to shake and shimmy and then Jade felt an unsettling heaviness as it lifted off. Through one of the side windows, she could see the emerald expanse of the Amazon basin falling away behind them.

Professor's voice sounded in Jade's headset. "Okay, now that we can hear ourselves think," he said, his tone even gruffer than usual, "maybe we can run through those introductions again, and then you can explain exactly how it is that you just happened to be out here. Your timing is a little suspicious."

"I'd say my timing was perfect," Kismet replied, evenly. "But you're right. As I said before, I was out here looking for..." He hesitated, glanced over at Jade. "For you."

"Right," Professor retorted, making no attempt

to hide his suspicion.

Or is it jealousy? She wondered.

"Okay, introductions take two," Kismet said. "I'm Nick. You're Jade. And you're... Sorry, I don't think I actually caught your name."

"Call me Pete." Professor narrowed his gaze at Kismet. "You're American. Are you a spook?"

Kismet shook his head. "No. I work for the UN. Specifically, for the Global Heritage Commission."

For the first time since meeting him, Jade felt a twinge of doubt. Maybe this wasn't a rescue after all.

The Global Heritage Commission was the enforcement arm of UNESCO—the United Nations Education Science and Cultural Organization. Jade didn't fully understand the political or bureaucratic intricacies of either body, but she was familiar with the mission of the former. GHC liaison agents worked with local law enforcement agencies to ensure the preservation of World Heritage sites and protect other unique cultural properties, which included random inspections of archaeological digs to ensure that the practices being used conformed to established guidelines and to expose illicit backdoor sales of artifacts to collectors.

"You work for the Global Heritage Commission and you're looking for me? Why? I haven't done anything wrong," Jade said, and then silently amended the statement, *Not lately anyway.*

"It's nothing like that," Kismet said, shaking his head emphatically. "Truthfully, I need your help with something. Something that has nothing to do with archaeology."

"If we refuse, are you going to kick us out?"

"Just hear me out."

Jade shrugged. "Go on."

"I understand that you had a hand in executing the estate of Gerald Roche."

Jade exchanged a wary glance with Professor.

Until his death, about a year earlier, Gerald Roche had been a notorious conspiracy celebrity and the author of several books about a purported takeover of global human society by what he called "changelings," so-named for the faerie creatures who substituted their own offspring for human children. There was some debate about whether Roche had actually believed that the changelings were supernatural creatures or merely a metaphor for the ruling elite, but after his murder, Jade and Professor had discovered a very real—and all too human— shadow government dating back several centuries. Roche himself was an odd character, and a notorious collector of occult memorabilia and other rare curiosities, which was how Jade had first become acquainted with him.

"Not exactly," she said, guardedly. "I was working with Dr. Allenby at the British Museum to preserve the collection intact, but the actual executors had other ideas. The provenance of most of the pieces was a bit dodgy—that was the word Dr. Allenby used—so we didn't put up too much of a fight. Most of the collection was sold at auction."

Kismet pursed his lips together in disappointment. "I'm specifically interested in a manuscript that might have been in his library. A book called the *Liber Arcanum*. Does that ring any bells?"

Professor leaned forward. "You're going to have to be a lot more specific than that. *Liber Arcanum* literally translates to 'Book of Secrets.' Every alchemist and occultist worth his salt wrote his own book of secrets, and I'd be willing to bet money that Gerald Roche had about a dozen of them."

Jade saw something change in Kismet's expression. His earlier confidence was gone, replaced by something that seemed almost like embarrassment or guilt. "As you might have already guessed, this gets into stuff that's a little… weird."

"We can handle weird," Jade said.

"If it involves Roche," Professor added, "that's pretty much a given."

Kismet nodded. "In April of 1904 an Englishman named Adam Garral climbed up the Great Pyramid at Giza in Egypt and spent the night inside the King's Chamber. Exactly what happened next is unclear, but when he emerged early the following day, he had in his possession a strange amulet which he claimed to have found in a hidden room deep within the pyramid—a room that no one else has ever found. He called the talisman 'the Apex,' probably because of its shape. It's a pyramid about so big." He held up his hand, finger and thumb spaced about three inches apart. "Made from a solid block of lapis lazuli, with what looks like a small skeletal hand gripping the exterior.

"Adam Garral was a minor occult figure in his day and it would be typical behavior for someone like that to concoct a wild origin story for a supposedly enchanted knick-knack, but for reasons I'm not prepared to go into right now, I think he was telling the truth."

"And you're trying to find this Apex," Jade guessed.

Kismet shook his head. "No. I already know where it is. I'm trying to figure out what happened next. Garral wrote in his diary that the Apex enabled him to, among other things, read a book he called 'the Liber Arcanum,' which was written in Enochian script. Enochian is a ciphertext language invented by Dr. John Dee and the magician Edward Kelley in the late 16th century, though they claimed it was actually the Angelic first language that mankind spoke before God confused the languages at the Tower of Babel."

"I've heard of it," Professor said, sending a wink in Jade's direction. "Despite that fanciful story, Enochian is remarkably similar to English in its grammatical structure and syntax."

Jade suppressed a giggle. "Most Americans think Jesus spoke English, so why not?"

Kismet frowned at the interruption, but pushed ahead with his story. "I'm not looking to prove

Garral's claims, but I do want to find out what happened to him. He found something in that book, and whatever it was caused him to leave England, after which his trail vanishes. The only lead I have right now is this *Liber Arcanum*."

"Which is written in Enochian," Jade said. "Enochian means John Dee, which brought you to Gerald Roche, which in turn brought you halfway around the world to me. You're going to an awful lot of trouble to find this guy."

Kismet shrugged. "I just missed you in Cuzco. Had to pull some strings to get the army to give me a ride out here."

"Lucky for us that you did." She stared at him a moment longer. "This isn't official business, is it? It's personal."

Kismet regarded her for several seconds then nodded. "Adam Garral was my great-great-grandfather."

Professor raised an eyebrow. "You're using your official capacity to investigate a personal matter?"

"If you're that worried about it," Kismet shot back, "I can always make this official. But that would mean billing you for the rescue."

Jade stifled a chuckle and held up her hands. "Okay, we're all friends here." She faced Kismet. "First, thank you for getting us out of there. Second... I'm sorry, I don't recall seeing anything called the Liber Arcanum at Gerald's place in

London, but that doesn't mean it wasn't there. If you'd like, I'd be happy to help you—"

"Jade," Professor said, his tone disapproving.

She waved him off and kept talking. "I'll put a call in to Kelly... Dr. Allenby. If she doesn't have it, she might know where it ended up."

"I appreciate it, but really there's no need for you to go to the trouble. You've already pointed me in the right direction. I'd hate to tear you away from your work here."

Jade glanced out the window again. The jungle looked deceptively peaceful from so high up. "I could go for a change of scenery. Oh, and a shower."

5

It was late evening before Jade and Professor managed to find a hotel room, procure some fresh clothes, and otherwise get cleaned up after the misadventure in the jungle. With a five-hour time difference between Cuzco and London, Jade knew it was already too late to reach Kelly Allenby at the British Museum, but she sent off a brief email, asking Allenby to call at her earliest convenience, before hitting the shower. She lingered there longer than she had intended, letting the hot water sweep away both the mud and grime, and the weariness of her post-adrenaline letdown.

When she felt vaguely human again, she toweled off, changed into her new clothes—nothing fancy, just a pair of dark green cargo shorts and a cream-colored tee with a silk-screened likeness of the Inca creator deity, Viracocha—and was just about to head down to the hotel restaurant to have dinner with Professor and Nick Kismet, when a knock sounded at her door. She peered through the peephole and saw Professor—likewise cleaned-up—waiting outside. He was alone and looked unusually pensive, fidgeting with his fedora which Jade noticed was now clean and restored to its original shape. Jade was accustomed to his gruff, almost dour manner, but she thought he looked even grumpier than usual.

She put on her best smile and threw the door

open. "Hey, I was just on my way down."

"We need to talk first." He made a "let me come in" gesture, and she stepped aside, allowing him to enter. He walked past her and sank into a chair.

Jade sat on the corner of the bed. "Why so glum, chum?"

Professor frowned. "I called Tam."

Tam was Tamara Broderick, an operations officer with the Central Intelligence Agency and leader of the Myrmidons. She was also the person who had assigned Professor to keep Jade out of trouble, which—if Jade was being honest—was pretty much a full-time job.

"Ah. Well, that's enough to put anyone in a bad mood," Jade retorted playfully.

"I thought I'd do a little background check on our mysterious savior."

Jade nodded slowly. Now Professor's mood made a bit more sense, but she still couldn't tell exactly what was bothering him. "And?"

"And, it seems that Nick Kismet is a bona fide hero. Served in army intelligence during the first Gulf War. He was involved in some kind of highly-classified op. Above top secret stuff. Sensitive Compartmented Information. Almost everything about him is SCI, and not even Tam has the clearance to read those files. All I could really dig up is what's on the Global Heritage Commission website. He's been with them since the mid-90s."

"He doesn't look that old."

"You'll have to ask him about that," Professor said curtly, then softened a degree or two. "You're right. He doesn't look a day over thirty. I don't know, maybe he found the Fountain of Youth or something."

Jade nodded absently, thinking that Professor sounded just the teensiest bit jealous of Nick Kismet.

Her relationship with Professor was unusual to say the least. He was her bodyguard and technically her assistant though she thought of him more as both an equal and a partner, even if his name didn't appear in the credits, so to speak. As a rule, letting things go from professional to personal was always a bad idea in a situation like that, but they had gone through too much together to be anything less than close friends. While she wasn't completely closed off to the idea of taking things to the next level, there was one other complication that neither of them had quite worked out.

Many years before, Professor had served in the SEALs with Dane Maddock—Jade's ex-boyfriend. Maddock was very much an ex, though there had been a few times when she had hoped things might break differently. She wanted to believe she was over him, but the feelings were still there, and for some perverse reason, the universe kept finding ways to remind her of them. Like arranging for her to work in close collaboration with one of Maddock's old teammates.

She probably could have dealt with that, but

she sensed it was a problem for Professor as well. Maybe dating a swim-buddy's ex was a violation of the "bro code" or something. and as near as she could tell, he wasn't ready to cross that line.

Sometimes that bothered her; it was like Dane Maddock was still interfering with her love life. Mostly though, she was just relieved that she didn't have to make a choice that would fundamentally alter their status quo.

Still, there was no reason for Professor to be feeling jealous or protective where Nick Kismet was concerned. It wasn't as if she was going to be working closely with the guy or anything.

"You don't trust him?"

Professor shrugged. "Oh, I trust that he's not an enemy of the United States."

He is *jealous*, she thought. "Then what's got your undies bunched?"

"Tam needs me in Washington."

Jade was taken aback. "Why?"

"Something to do with Maddock's friend Jimmy Letson. She wasn't able to go into much detail, but it sounds like he's gone off the grid and that has her spooked. She's got her hands full with something else, so she asked me to look into it."

"When do we leave?"

He shook his head. "Tam wants you to stay here and work with Kismet."

"Uh, in case you've forgotten, I don't work for Tam."

The faintest hint of a smile flickered across Professor's face, but just as quickly vanished, replaced by the same irritated frown that had first greeted her. "Well, I can't make you work with him, but you can't come with me. I *do* work for Tam, and she told me to leave you behind." He paused a beat before adding, "She made it very clear that it would be in everyone's best interests if you helped him. She would owe you a favor."

Jade wagged her head sideways in a "whatever" gesture, but she secretly was pleased at the idea of Tam Broderick owing her a favor. "So I'm just supposed to chill here until you get back?"

"Here. Or wherever the search takes you. But to answer your original question, I'm heading to the airport now."

"What? What about dinner?"

"Rain check. Besides, three's a crowd." He shrugged. "I'd tell you to take care of yourself, but you never listen anyway. But if it's any consolation, from what I've read—maybe it would be more accurate to say, from what I haven't read—I think you'll be in good hands."

He stopped abruptly as if realizing too late how awkward the comment sounded, then rose to his feet and headed for the door. "Gotta go," he muttered, shoving his hat onto his head. "Taxi's waiting."

6

The restaurant maître d' escorted Jade to the table where Nick Kismet was seated. Jade appraised him as she made her approach. He still wore the same casual attire as before, yet there was something different about him. It took her a second to realize what it was, and by that time, she was standing across from him.

He rose to greet her, retaking his chair only after she had taken hers. As he did, he turned to the waiter and gestured to the empty rocks glass on the table. "Another for me. And the lady will have…?" He glanced at Jade.

Jade couldn't decide if Kismet was trying to be a gentleman or if he was naturally pushy, nor could she decide how she felt about it. "The lady will have Dos Equis if you've got it."

The waiter gave a helpless shrug. "*Lo siento.*" Then he added in accented but passable English. "We have Budweiser."

Jade made a face. "Great. Got anything local?"

"*Si.* We have a Ayrampo Roja—red ale—on draft from Cerveceria del Valle Sagrado. It is very popular with international visitors."

Jade looked back at Kismet. "What are you drinking?"

"Twelve-year-old Macallan. But I'm willing to live dangerously if you are."

"Ha. Okay. Let's do it."

Kismet flashed what she could only describe as a roguish grin and then turned back to the waiter. *"Tenemos dos, por favor."*

As the waiter moved off, Kismet faced Jade. "I wouldn't have taken you for a beer drinker," he said.

In truth, she wasn't. When she drank, which wasn't often, it was usually in social situations and she would drink whatever was put in front of her, knocking back pints or shots as if to prove she could hold her own with any grad student or former Navy SEAL. She had picked up a taste for Dos Equis when she and Maddock had been an item, and she still defaulted to it for old-time's sake, which was probably a sign of weakness on her part.

Still, where did Kismet get off making assumptions about her?

"Shows what you know." She paused a moment, then said. "You got a haircut."

His mouth twitched into something that wasn't quite a smile, then he shrugged and changed the subject. "Where's your friend? Skipper, wasn't it?"

"Very funny. It's Professor, but you can call him Dr. Chapman. Or you could have, if he hadn't been called away on other business." She hesitated, feeling Professor's absence even more acutely. *God, this is like being set up on a blind date.* "He's a SEAL, you know," she added with perhaps more assertiveness than the situation called for. "And he's got friends in very high places. He checked up on you before he left,"

"Is that a fact?"

"Damn straight. I know all about you, Nick Kismet."

"And yet you're still here," he said, laughing. The waiter arrived a moment later with two pint glasses filled with amber colored liquid. Kismet regarded her across the table for a moment then looked up at the waiter. "We'll need a few more minutes, I think."

When they were alone again, he continued. "So, if you know all about me, I guess we'll have to come up with something else to talk about. You, for instance."

Jade now regretted the hasty comment since, in fact, she knew almost nothing about him, but before she could think of a retort, her phone began buzzing. She dug it out of her pocket, hoping against hope that it would be Professor calling to let her know that his plans had changed and he was already on his way back, but it wasn't him; it was Kelly Allenby.

She hit the button to accept the call. "Kelly. What are you still doing up? It must be after midnight there."

Allenby's laughing voice filled her ear. "Jim took me to the cinema, and drinks after. I only just saw your email."

"You didn't have to get back to me right away," Jade said. "It's nothing that can't wait until morning."

"No need to wait. It's a simple request with a

simple answer."

Jade didn't like the sound of that. A simple answer in this case probably meant they were out of luck. She noticed Kismet watching her intently. "Kelly, I'm here with…uh, Nick. Nick Kismet. Can I put you on speaker?"

"Certainly."

Jade set the phone on the table and tapped the touch-screen to activate speaker mode. Kismet leaned over. "Dr. Allenby, I'm Nick Kismet with the Global Heritage Commission."

"Please, call me Kelly. I've heard a lot about you, Mr. Kismet."

Kismet chuckled. "I'm getting that a lot today."

"Jade says that you're looking for a manuscript from the estate of Gerald Roche, written in Enochian script, called *Liber Arcanum*, possibly authored by John Dee or Edward Kelley. Is that right?"

"Pretty close."

"The museum wasn't able to acquire all of Mr. Roche's library, but we were able to scan everything before the collection was released for auction. We have a virtual copy of every rare book or manuscript in his collection. Now, there's good news and bad. The bad is that there's nothing explicitly identified as *Liber Arcanum*. But there are several manuscripts that haven't been identified yet, so it's possible that one of them is what you're looking for."

"That is good news," Kismet said, with a

genuine smile.

"I'll email Jade the link to the online archive. You can view the scans at your leisure."

Jade could see that Kismet was eager to get started. "Thanks so much, Kelly," she said. "I thought we were going to have to travel there in person."

"Oh, I wish you would. I'd love to see you again and catch up. And I wouldn't mind a chance to meet you in person too, Mr. Kismet."

"If you ever do," Kismet replied, "You'd better call me Nick."

Jade thanked Allenby again, and then rang off to check her email. The link was there, as promised, but when Jade clicked through and began selecting files to view, she realized the limitations of the technology. The crabbed handwriting was indecipherable in normal view, and when she tried to zoom in, she had to scroll back and forth to read complete lines. Not that she could actually read the odd script, which looked a little like Greek.

"You're going to need that Apex thingy if you want to read this," she remarked.

Kismet shifted in his chair, suddenly looking a little nervous. "There are online translation tools that can help with that," he said. "And I'm good with languages. Even made up ones."

"Hmm. We're going to need a bigger screen."

"I've got a tablet computer in my room," Kismet said. "That should make it easier to view the scans." He paused a beat before adding. "You said 'we.'"

"Yeah. Why? Were you planning to kick me to the curb?"

"Not at all. I just assumed that you—"

"Yeah, well you know what happens when you assume." She took a long pull from her beer, then brought the glass down a little more forcefully than she had intended. "I vote we order room service, and move this party to your place."

She allowed herself a small smile when she noticed that, under his thick beard, Nick Kismet was blushing.

7

"**Party,**" **Jade decided,** wasn't the right word for what happened next. It was more like… Well, work. But Kismet's room was quieter than the restaurant, and so far, he had been a perfect gentleman.

Maybe a little too perfect. Jade wouldn't have minded catching him sneaking an appraising glance at her once in a while, but his attention was entirely consumed with the images from the British Museum online archive.

The larger screen on Kismet's tablet computer did make it easier to *see* the scans, but did not make them any less incomprehensible. Worse, as Kismet opened one file after another, flipping through the documents like they were pages in a retail catalog, he seemed to lose all interest in conversation.

"Are you sure you haven't got one of those Apex thingies?" she asked after a while.

He looked up, blinking several times as if trying to relieve eye strain. "What?"

"You haven't used any of those online resources you were talking about. From where I'm sitting, it looks like your sight-reading this stuff." Even as she said it aloud, she realized that was exactly what he was doing. "Oh, my God. You do have it, don't you?"

"I… It's not like that," he said, a little too quickly. "I'm not reading it, I'm just trying to get an overview."

"Bull crap," Jade fired back. "You're reading it. You've got the Apex stone, don't you?"

Kismet sighed, then reached up to the collar of his shirt and tugged it down to reveal a pendant dangling from a rawhide strip around his neck. It was exactly as he had described it, a pyramid of dark blue lapis lazuli flecked with gold pyrite and white calcite, with ridges that looked exactly like the bones of a child's hand fused in place as if gripping it.

"Can I try it?"

Kismet didn't react visibly, but Jade could tell that the question discomfited him. She had a mental image of Smeagol from Lord of the Rings, lovingly clutching the ring and whispering "Precious," and decided not to press the issue. "How does it work? Is it automatic? Like a universal translator?"

"I'm not really sure that it's doing anything," Kismet admitted. "I told you I was good with languages. It wasn't an exaggeration. I've looked at a lot of this writing since I started looking for the *Liber Arcanum*. At first, it was hard to decipher, but now…" He shrugged. "The script looks exactly the same, but it just sort of makes sense to me."

"But you're actually reading this?"

"Skimming it. I've seen most of this stuff before in other editions, so what I'm really doing is looking for something different. Something that…"

He trailed off, prompting Jade to take another look at the screen. The image on the screen was more of the same—strange Enochian glyphs, the so-called Angelic language—but they were not broken up into words or discrete lines. Instead, the arrangement looked more like a word search puzzle, with each individual character evenly spaced in relation to the next, to form a grid—Jade's best guess was that it was a fifty-by-fifty grid. The script remained unreadable to her, but Jade thought she could see intentional patterns, as if the strange letters had been used to produce a picture. But that wasn't the really weird part.

There were words written on the page, outside the grid. English words. Comments, with little arrows drawn to underlined portions of the text. Without context, the comments themselves were just as cryptic. There were references to elements and directions, and names that sounded like Latin words, followed by numerical notations that might have been page or chapters numbers.

Kismet had not said a word for what seemed like several minutes. "Is this it? Is this the one?"

"This is the *Liber Loagaeth*," he said, speaking slowly.

"What does that mean? Is it, or isn't it the book you're looking for?"

"The name means 'Book of the Speech of God' but it's sometimes also called '*Liber Mysteriorum.*' 'Book of Mysteries.' Edward Kelley composed it based on a revelation he claimed to have received after looking into John Dee's crystal Shew Stone."

Jade coughed nervously. "Never heard of it."

"The book itself is fairly well known, but there's no definitive translation. This is a hand-written copy. It was a fairly standard practice for occult students to write one in their own hand. I think this one belonged to Adam Garral. That's his writing in the margins."

"Get out." Jade slugged him playfully in the shoulder.

Kismet grinned, but then resumed clicking through the pages with renewed enthusiasm. Each new page was a different grid, with even more elaborate—and clearly intentional—patterns, and on each were more notes. Kismet seemed to devour them all in a single glance, not even giving Jade enough time to read the scribbled comments. Then, for no apparent reason, he lingered on one page, reading it several times. Finally, he offered an explanation.

"This page…it's different than the other versions."

"Different how?"

"There's a mention here of the smoking mirror which shows the past and the future. I'm paraphrasing of course. It's widely believed that Dee and Kelley used both crystals—like the Shew Stone—and an obsidian scrying mirror obtained in the New World, but this is the first time I've seen an explicit reference to it. In this passage, the angel is recounting how the mirror was found in the temple of someone named…" He paused. "Well, that's odd. It just says the 'pyramid temple of smoking mirror.'"

"Not so odd," Jade said. "The Aztec deity of divination was named Tezcatlipoca, which literally translates to 'smoking mirror.' He was the god of, among other things, obsidian. Obsidian mirrors are a common artifact found in his temples."

"Okay, that makes sense. What's really strange is that I've never seen mention of the mirror in any of Dee's writings."

Jade nodded, recalling a conversation about the topic with Kelly Allenby at the British Museum. Although several crystal balls and other items were associated with Dee and his divination attempts, none of those objects had been reliably proven to have ever belonged to him.

"The angel talks about showing distant lands and things to come," Kismet continued, "and promises to show the seer how to find the other elemental temples."

"What does that mean?"

Kismet shook his head and swiped his finger across the tablet to bring up the next document. Jade gasped in disbelief. The document was not written in Enochian script, nor did it appear to have ever been a part of the grimoire. It was a letter, written on a piece of stationery that bore the letterhead: "BRITISH ANTARCTIC EXPEDITION 1910, 36 & 38 VICTORIA STREET, LONDON S.W."

The missive written to a certain Capt. J.E. Grace, was both a note of thanks, for a contribution in the amount of £1,000, and of congratulations, praising Captain Grace's expertise with horses and welcoming him to the expedition. It was signed, "Your faithful servant, R. Scott."

In the blank space at the top of the page, someone—the same someone that had made notes in the margins of the occult manuscript—had written: "Poor Scott. He thinks he'll find immortality at the Pole, but I've got the map! VITRIOL!"

"One of these things is not like the other," Jade said, shaking her head as she read the letter a second time. There was an accompanying notation from the archivist, indicating that the letter had been discovered between two pages of the folio, and was included in the file exactly as it had been found. "What do you suppose that's doing there?"

Kismet just stared at the screen for several moments in silent contemplation. Finally, he shook his head. "Unbelievable."

"What's unbelievable?"

He pointed to the screen. "This letter. Do you know what it is?"

Jade shook her head uncertainly. "Antarctic expedition…1910…Scott. Kind of rings a bell."

She was acutely feeling Professor's absence now. He would have already launched into a thorough explanation of the letter's significance.

"Robert Falcon Scott was a British naval officer and polar explorer. He wanted to be the first man to reach the South Pole. That's what this expedition was all about. He made it to the pole, though another expedition led by Roald Amundsen beat him there by a month. Scott and his team all died on the return trip. This man—Captain John Edward Grace—was with him almost to the end. According to Scott's diary, Grace suffering from frostbite and scurvy, left the tent and walked out into a blizzard so that the others wouldn't waste any more resources on him. Supposedly, the last thing he said was, 'I am just going outside and may be some time.' His sacrifice ultimately didn't matter because Scott and the others only made it another twenty miles before getting stopped in their tracks by the storm. They all starved to death."

"Okay," Jade said slowly. "And this is important why?" Silently, she added, *Professor, where are you when I need you?*

Kismet took a deep breath and let it out. "I think Adam Garral and Captain Grace were one and the same."

"You think?" Jade said, enunciating the words like an accusation. "He's your great-grandfather. Don't you know? I mean, you look it up on Ancestry.com, yeah?"

Kismet's face screwed up in a look that was part-annoyance and part-reservation. "Until recently, I never had a reason to investigate the family lore. I was told that Garral was something of a wandering libertine. Even his relationship with his wife, my great-great-grandmother, was an unconventional one; something to do with an occult rite if I understand correctly. He was always off on some adventure or another, and while he would write from time to time, it wasn't like he could send GPS tagged photos from his smartphone. All she really had was his word for it. And when he disappeared in 1910, she just assumed he was off on another adventure. But aside from the oral tradition, there's really not a lot of information about him. It's not impossible… No, scratch that. It's entirely plausible that he was leading a double life."

"Okay, but this other guy, Grace, he's a known historical quantity."

"Good point." Kismet closed the browser window displaying the letter and opened a search engine, into which he typed in the name of the polar explorer.

John Edward Grace had been born in 1880 to a landed family in London. Although the family occupied the manor hall at Gestingthorpe near Sudbury, Grace spent his school years in Putney, London and then attended Eton College, though he did not complete his studies there. He only had one sibling—a sister—and his father died when Grace was just sixteen. Perhaps inspired by his uncle, a famed explorer and naturalist, Grace embarked on a military career, which took him to the far-flung corners of the empire—South Africa, India, Egypt— where he was commended for bravery and ultimately promoted to the rank of captain. In 1910, he took an interest in joining Scott's expedition, buying his way onto the competitive roster with a sizeable monetary donation, though according to Scott, it was Grace's expertise with horses that was the deciding factor. Most of Scott's team was composed of close acquaintances and polar veterans from Shackleton's expeditions, with Grace being a rare outsider.

The relationship between the two men was tense at times, with Grace complaining about Scott's leadership, but Scott nevertheless included him in the five-man team that set out on the final push to plant the Union Jack at the South Pole. Unfortunately for them, when they arrived, they found a tent left behind by Amundsen along with a letter dated thirty-five days earlier. Even worse, owing to increasingly difficult weather conditions and injuries—including a fall that killed one member of the team—the return trip took longer than expected and the dog-sled teams that were supposed to meet them never showed up. The men quickly ran out of supplies, which led to further health complications. Grace, suffering from scurvy which may have aggravated an old war injury, soon succumbed to frostbite and gangrene, and knowing that his death was looming, left the tent and vanished forever into history. His famous parting words may have been apocryphal, but embodied a bold and self-sacrificing spirit.

And yet, there was clearly more to the man than history realized. For nearly a century, it was believed that Grace had died without offspring, but a 2002 biography offered compelling evidence that Grace had fathered a child out of wedlock, with a 12-year-old Scottish girl.

"That takes sowing wild oats to a new low," Jade remarked.

"You know if he lived one secret life, maybe he had another; one that nobody knows about."

"That would be a scandalous revelation, even today. It sounds like this guy is still a national hero."

Kismet nodded slowly. "I'm not interested in rewriting the history books. I just want to know what happened to him." He paused. "Adam Garral left the Apex with his wife and infant son, and if he and Grace were really the same person, then we know where he went. But why?"

Jade snapped her fingers. "The note scribbled on that letter. It said something about immortality."

Kismet clicked back to the document and read the handwritten note aloud. "'Poor Scott. He thinks he'll find immortality at the Pole, but I've got the map! VITRIOL!'"

"Vitriol? That's some kind of acid, yeah?"

Kismet nodded. "It's an archaic term for sulfate. But it's also an acronym for the motto of medieval alchemists. *Visita Interiora Terrae Rectificando Invenies Occultum Lapidem.* 'Visit the interior of the earth and rectifying you will find the secret stone.'"

"Oooh, there's a secret stone. Interior of the

earth? Does that mean a cave, or are we talking hollow earth theory?"

"For the alchemists, it was probably the latter. And the secret stone was a reference to the Philosopher's Stone which could supposedly transmute base metals into gold or even make a person immortal."

"Immortality," Jade said. "Scott was looking for the immortality of fame, but Grace—or Garral—was looking for the real deal, and the map he had led him to the South Pole."

"Most hollow earth theories held that there were openings to the interior world at the poles. Even as late as the 1950s, some of these scientific expeditions were actually looking for an entrance." Kismet tapped his fingers on the table, deep in thought. "You know what? I think the name 'Garral' is another clue?"

"How so?"

"Garral is a very uncommon surname, but it was used by Jules Verne in the novel *Eight Hundred Leagues on the Amazon*."

"And Jules Verne wrote *Journey to the Center of the Earth*," Jade said, catching on.

"Something my great-great grandfather read in the *Liber Arcanum* convinced him he could find an entrance to the interior world in Antarctica. I think he was being literal when he said he had a map."

"I guess it led him astray."

"Maybe. Or maybe he never got the chance to

go looking for it on his own. Maybe that's what he was trying to do at the end."

"You think Scott was lying about his condition? Frostbite and gangrene?"

"Probably not. Maybe at that point, he was delusional. If he was, the map is probably still with his body." Kismet stared at the screen for a long time. "We need to find him. His remains, I mean."

Jade grimaced. "Umm, you're kidding, right? You're talking about finding a needle in an Antarctica-sized haystack."

"Not necessarily. Scott recorded the exact coordinates of the camp where Grace vanished. Assuming that he really was suffering from frostbite, he wouldn't have gotten far."

"Maybe not, but it's been over a hundred years. That spot is probably buried under a ton of ice."

"Probably," Kismet agreed. "But with modern technology, I think we can definitely shrink the haystack down to something a little more manageable."

"We?"

"I thought you would want to see this through. Unless you're planning to kick *me* to the curb," Kismet said, throwing her earlier words back at her.

"That was before you said anything about Antarctica." Jade shivered just thinking about it. But, she also recalled what Professor had said about sticking close to Kismet. She let out a growl of defeat, but before she could articulate the terms of her surrender, a knock came at the door, followed by a loud female voice: "Room service."

"Took them long enough," Jade muttered, though secretly she was grateful for the interruption. It would give her a few seconds to think of something better to say to Kismet. She pushed out of her chair and started for the door. "I'll get it."

She reached the door in a few quick steps and, after checking the peephole to make sure that the woman on the other side of the door was indeed wearing the attire of a hotel server and pushing a tray-laden cart, threw the door wide.

"Perfect timing," she started to say, but the cheery greeting turned to a yelp of alarm as, first one, then a pair, then four men, who had been lined up along the wall, just outside the peephole's periphery, surged toward her.

8

Kismet was on his feet in an instant, but the intruders had the initiative. They also had guns—large semi-automatic pistols—which they trained on Kismet and Jade. One of the men grabbed Jade by the arm and pushed her back into the room.

Jade's first thought was the men who had pursued her and Professor through the rain forest had somehow tracked her here, intending to finish what they had started earlier. It was a reasonable conclusion; the men were a rough-looking bunch and with their dark hair and swarthy complexions, they might have passed for locals. But when the fifth member of the group—the woman pushing the room service cart—stepped right past Jade and stalked toward Kismet, Jade realized they weren't here for her at all.

The woman was strikingly beautiful. Her long glossy black hair framed an angular face with an olive complexion and high cheekbones; Mediterranean features, Jade decided, or possibly Arabian. She now saw that the server's jacket hung loose on the woman's frame, as if several sizes too big; no doubt borrowed from an actual hotel employee. The woman strode into the room with the confidence of a runway model, stopping when she was almost face-to-face with Kismet. Jade had only an oblique view of the confrontation, but she could see the anger radiating from the woman's coal black eyes.

"You have something that belongs to me," the woman said. Her voice was about what Jade expected, smooth and melodious, and decidedly at odds with the menace that dripped from every consonant.

Kismet, who had his hands raised, regarded her with thoughtful wariness. "I think you've got the wrong room."

She stared back at him for several seconds, then gave him a cold smile. "No, Nick Kismet. I am exactly where I want to be."

Okay, Jade thought. *Definitely not here for me.*

Although her heart was pounding like crazy, she willed herself calm, took a deep breath and cleared her throat. "Well you two obviously have some catching up to do," she said, trying to inject some bravado into her tone to mask just how terrified she was. "I'll leave you to it."

And with that, she pivoted toward the exit. The move took her captor by surprise, and before he could react, she twisted out of his grip.

Jade wasn't sure what she was trying to accomplish. On one level, she thought the intruders might just let her go. Unlikely, she knew, but not impossible. High-stress situations sometimes did funny things to people. Maybe they would be so focused on Kismet that they wouldn't know how to react until she was already in the clear.

And if that happened, what then? Should she

run for it? Call for help? Pull the fire alarm, maybe?

It was a moot question. The man wasn't about to let her leave the room. He twisted around and made a grab for her, which was, after all, what she had actually been expecting him to do.

From the moment the gunmen barged into the room, Jade had started mentally reviewing all the self-defense lessons she had ever received. Maddock had taught her a few moves, and Professor had built on that foundation with semi-formal instruction in grappling and basic martial arts. One thing he had said now came back to her; just two words: *Don't hesitate.*

In a potential hostage-taking scenario, Professor had told her, the longer you waited, hoping for someone to come along and save you, the more control you gave to your would-be captor. It was important to act quickly and decisively before those roles—hostage and captor—became fixed, hardening like concrete. Jade had remembered that lesson, forcing herself to act, to move, to do something...anything... before that deadly inertia could set in.

The rest was almost automatic.

She allowed the man to seize her forearm, but as he did, she sidestepped into his weak side, performing an aikido combination known as *Irimi Nage*—the entering throw. She moved in close, almost spooning him from behind, and got her free hand up onto his neck, pushing him in the direction he was already traveling. She could feel his astonishment in the tightening of his muscles, the immediate reflexive resistance. Professor had taught her to be ready for that, too. As the man shifted, trying to brace himself, she shifted too, whirling him around, unbalancing him completely.

Even as she launched into the almost choreographed routine, the rest of the intruders began reacting as well, but Jade's decisiveness had deprived them of the initiative. They still had the numbers, but for the moment, she was calling the shots. Guns swiveled around and were aimed uncertainly in her direction. What were they supposed to do now? Shoot her? That wasn't the plan. Almost in unison, they looked to their leader, the striking woman who had been in the process of confronting Kismet, only to discover that situation had undergone a similarly dramatic change.

"Guns down!" Kismet barked.

Jade finished the throw, putting the gunman on his back, hard enough to knock the wind out of him, and glanced up just in time to see Kismet whirl the woman around so that she was facing the other men. He had his left arm securely around her waist, and his right snaked up under her right armpit to press something to her throat.

It was a knife, but that description seemed inadequate. Jade was reminded of a scene from an old movie—*Crocodile Dundee*—where the Aussie hero, threatened by a mugger with a switchblade, laughingly says, "That's not a knife," and then, drawing a wicked-looking ten-inch long Bowie knife, finishes with, "*That's* a knife."

Kismet's weapon of choice wasn't a Bowie knife, but something even bigger, and perhaps just a touch more wicked-looking. It was a *kukri*, the signature weapon of the fierce Gurkha warriors from Nepal. The blade had an odd boomerang shape, with the cutting edge on the inside of the elbow-like bend. Jade had seen similar knives, variations on the same style, but the knife Kismet held looked less refined than most she had seen, rougher, more authentic somehow, and Jade couldn't help but think that it had probably spilled more than a little actual blood.

She also wondered where he had been hiding it.

"Guns down." Kismet repeated in a flat tone. "Or she dies."

The gunmen all looked to the woman—Kismet's hostage—taking their cues from her, and she evidently wasn't ready to submit. "You're outnumbered, Kismet," she hissed. "If you kill me, you will certainly die."

She had an oddly formal manner of speech and an accent that suggested English might not be her first language.

"Don't bet your life on that," Kismet said, and then directing his gaze at the gunmen, added. "Don't bet *her* life on it. Put the guns down." Then, before they could accede or refuse, he snapped.

"Jade, come over here now."

Jade lurched into motion, hurrying over to stand behind Kismet before any of the gunmen could even think about trying to grab her in order to balance the terms of the standoff.

Not that she would have submitted easily.

She recognized that he was doing the same thing she had. Reacting, moving, refusing to get bogged down in inertia. She got close to him, turning so that they were back to back.

The woman started to say something, another defiant threat perhaps, but Kismet silenced her with a rough shake and growled in her ear. "Tell them to drop their guns, or you will bleed."

"Do as he says," she said, her voice tight.

One by one, the gunmen lowered their guns. They did not drop them, but aimed them at the floor, as if testing Kismet's resolve.

It was a mistake.

The woman let out a wail as the blade bit into the flesh under her throat. Almost simultaneously, the pistols began thudding on the carpet.

"That's better," Kismet said. "Now, get in the bathroom."

The men hesitated, so Kismet dug the blade of the kukri in again until the woman whimpered. "Do it!"

The men grudgingly filed into the small lavatory room and, without being told to do so, closed the door.

"Get their guns," Kismet said to Jade.

Jade hurried forward and collected the weapons, holding them with the same kind of caution she might have used holding a snake. "What should I do with them?"

He shrugged. "Think of something."

She dumped them on the room service cart, and then picked up the domed tray cover and used it to conceal them. "Cool. What now?"

"Grab my tablet. And then get ready to move. We're getting out of here in a minute. But first…" He moved his knife away from the woman's throat but did not release her. There was a two-inch long red line on the skin below her jaw, slowly oozing tears of blood. "Who are you?" he hissed. "And what the hell do you want?"

She made a noise in her throat, as if trying to gather enough saliva to spit. "You killed my husband. And I am going to kill you."

"I've killed a lot of husbands," Kismet retorted. "You'll have to do better than that."

Jade felt an ominous chill at his casual admission.

He's kidding, right?

She looked away quickly so her face would not betray her, and grabbed the tablet off the table, tucking it under one arm.

"His name was Alexander Cerulean," the woman hissed.

Kismet nodded slowly. "And you are?"

"Aliyah."

"Okay, listen to me Aliyah. I get that you think you need to avenge your beloved, but that's not going to happen. Get over it. Go home and move on with your life. If you don't, I promise you'll join your husband in hell. This is your only warning."

Then, to punctuate the ultimatum, he drew back his hand and hammered the butt end of the kukri into the back of her head.

Aliyah Cerulean crumpled to the floor.

Kismet whirled to face Jade. "Go! Get the elevator."

Jade threw the door open and raced into the hallway, with Kismet right behind her. She sprinted to the elevator foyer, punched the call button and then looked back to see if any of Aliyah's men were giving chase. There was no sign of pursuit, but Jade knew that might change at any second. She looked back at the elevators, checked the indicators above each set of doors. The hotel had only five floors, and Kismet's room was on the third, so they shouldn't have had to wait more than a few seconds, but like the proverbial watched pot, it seemed to take forever. Finally, there was a loud chime as one of the cars arrived, and a moment after that, the doors slid open.

She started to go inside, but Kismet held her back. "Not this one," he said. He leaned head and shoulders inside the car, punched a button on the panel, and then drew back before the doors could close. He then pivoted away, rounding a corner and heading down an adjacent hallway. "Come on."

"What the hell are you—?" Kismet was gone before Jade could finish the question, so she hurried to catch up to him. She caught up to him just as he was entering a door at the far end of the hallway; the placard beside it showed a graphical representation of someone descending a staircase.

Stairs, Jade thought. *What the hell is he doing?*

To her further consternation, instead of heading down toward the exit, Kismet began ascending. Jade didn't even bother to ask, but hurried after him.

When he reached the next landing, Kismet pushed through the door and headed down the corridor, moving at a fast walk, too fast for Jade to simultaneously walk and talk. She could barely contain her ire when he arrived at what appeared to be his ultimate destination: the elevator foyer.

"Are you kidding me?" She snarled. "Why didn't we just—?"

He touched a finger to his lips. "Shhh."

"Don't shush me," she shot back, though in a considerably lower voice.

Kismet just pointed to the indicator. The one above the door to the car she had summoned earlier showed that it was now in the lobby. The elevator beside it was rising, responding to someone else's call.

It stopped on the third floor.

Jade frowned. She was starting to grasp Kismet's overall intent, but that didn't mean she was prepared to forgive him for not including her.

God, she thought. *He's even more annoying than Maddock.*

Another thirty seconds passed, and then the indicator changed to "2" and kept going.

Kismet let out the breath he had been holding. "I think they took the bait. Now they can chase their tail for a while trying to figure out where we went."

"So, you never had any intention of leaving the hotel?"

"Oh, we're leaving. But not until we're good and ready."

"'We' again? You're making a lot of assumptions, Nick Kismet."

"You're right." He inclined his head in a deferential bow. "Thanks for your help, Dr. Ihara. It's been a pleasure working with you. I'll send you a postcard from Antarctica."

"And now you're assuming that I *don't* want to go with you," she shot back. "Why don't you try asking?"

A mischievous smile formed on his lips. "Okay. Dr. Ihara, I'm going to Antarctica. Would you care to join me?"

She stared back at him, her eyes hard as diamonds. "That woman, Aliyah… Did you really kill her husband?"

His smile slipped a notch. "A few weeks ago, Alexander Cerulean stole the Apex from my father. I tracked him to Cairo, to the Great Pyramid. He…"

Kismet hesitated a moment. "We struggled and he fell. It was self-defense."

"Yeah? You do that a lot?"

He uttered a short, humorless laugh. "More than I care to admit." He paused a beat, then added, "Speaking of self-defense, you handled yourself pretty well back there."

"Thanks."

"Look, I'm sorry that you got dragged into this."

"It happens." She shrugged. "So, Antarctica, huh? Gonna be cold, yeah?"

Kismet nodded. "Yeah.

PART TWO: MADDOCK

9

Antarctica

"Back up a second," Dane Maddock said, holding up his hands, palms out. "Jimmy's in trouble?"

Jade frowned, evidently irritated at the interruption of her narrative, and for a few seconds, the only sound was the soft murmur of Ivan's engine vibrating through the vehicle, and crunch of the heavy-duty monster-truck sized tires compressing ice crystals on the frozen road that linked the airstrip to the permanent installation of McMurdo Station.

Ivan was not "some dude" as Bones had suggested. That mystery had been cleared up as soon as the large red and white all-terrain all-weather multi-passenger vehicle had pulled up beside them. Painted in big block letters on the front fender of the enormous shuttle were the words: "'Ivan' the Terra Bus."

Jade finally glanced over at Kismet. "Maybe you should field this one."

Kismet nodded. "As near as we can put together, when you asked your friend, Mr. Letson, to look into the mystery of that plane wreck you found in South Africa, it tripped some kind of silent alarm and put both you and him on Prometheus' radar."

A few days earlier, Maddock and his crew of

underwater treasure hunters had found the sunken wreckage of what appeared to be an old *Boeing 314 Clipper*—an enormous flying boat built just before World War II. What made the discovery unusual was the fact that there was neither a record of such a plane crashing there, nor of the plane's actual existence. Only a handful of planes from that line had been built, and all of them were accounted for. Jimmy had made a few discreet inquiries, none of which had really helped much, and that had seemingly been the end of that.

Except, immediately afterward, Jimmy had gone incommunicado. Then a group of mysterious killers had made, not one but several attempts on their lives as they slowly pieced together the story of the mystery clipper's final flight. The trail had led them to Antarctica where they had discovered the strange orb in the frozen pyramid their new traveling companion Rose Greer had dubbed 'the Outpost,' but until Jade and Kismet had arrived, swooping down out of the sky to scatter the attacking enemy, Maddock did not know who was behind it all. Nor had he realized that Jimmy had been caught up in the web as well.

Now he had a name to attach to the killers who had pursued him. Prometheus.

"Jimmy's safe by the way," Jade added. "He's with Professor. They're the ones who figured out that Prometheus was coming after you down here. Since we were close, Tam asked us to come bail you out. Lucky, yeah?"

Dane Maddock wasn't a big believer in luck. He faced Kismet. "You seem to be the expert on Prometheus. Who or what are they?"

Kismet took a moment to consider his answer. "Jade has told me about some of your… ah, adventures? So I know that you'll understand what I mean when I say that there are… things. Objects. Artifacts and relics, and such, that are *powerful.*"

"Oh, brother," Bones said, wagging his head. "You would not believe some of the crap we've seen."

"I think I might at that," Kismet said. "The short answer to your question is that Prometheus is a secret society dedicated to controlling those objects of power. Not just controlling them, but erasing them from history. They think they're doing us all a favor. That human society isn't ready for the truth about… Well, everything. Gods and devils, aliens…You name it, they want to keep it a secret. They chose Prometheus the Titan—the god of foresight—as their mascot, because he tried to protect mankind from the games played by the gods. That's what they think they are doing."

"Sounds very paternalistic," Maddock said. "And arrogant."

"I don't know," Bones countered. "People are pretty stupid. I mean, I don't trust our government with some of the stuff we've found, and ours is better than most."

Kismet gave an ambivalent shrug. "You're not wrong about their arrogance. They recruit only the best and brightest. The intellectual elite. Which makes them particularly formidable. And their wall of secrecy is all but impenetrable."

"You evidently penetrated it."

Kismet grimaced. "I have a… call it an inside source. But even so, I've only scratched the surface. What I do know is that in the last few years there's been a schism. One faction supports the original mission, the long game. The other side has more of a use-it-or-lose-it philosophy. The latter group is weaker but desperate enough to go for the nuclear option."

"Do you mean that literally?" Bones asked.

"Maybe. My source told me that orb you found—the anomaly—has been on their hit list for a while." He glanced at Rose, who carried the strange black sphere in a backpack slung over one shoulder. "When Mr. Letson's inquiry got flagged, the splinter faction realized somebody was looking for it and decided to make their power play."

Bones nodded slowly, and then articulated what Maddock was thinking. "Helluva coincidence that you—the expert on Prometheus—just happened to be here on unrelated business."

Kismet rubbed his bearded chin. "I'm not so sure it's unrelated after all."

"What a surprise," Bones chuckled.

Maddock reflected on the story Jade had recounted to them. "You're thinking that this relative of yours, Garral... Grace. He was looking for what we found?"

"It's certainly possible, though based on what we know of Scott's expedition, he never got anywhere close to the valley where you found the Outpost. But if there was a pre-historic civilization down here, there could well be other outposts just like it buried under the ice."

"That's consistent with the stories my great-grandad wrote," put in Rose Greer. Rose, a history professor from upstate New York, had found the solution to the mystery of the Clipper wreck in the pages of a pulp novel written by her great-grandfather, David "Dodge" Dalton. and ultimately guided Maddock and Bones to the Outpost.

"It's possible that Grace-Garral was looking for the anomaly," Kismet said. "But I think the anomaly is part of something bigger. Garral mentioned a map. I think the anomaly might be a compass, pointing the way to something else. But we'll know for sure when we find his remains and see the map for ourselves."

"About that," Maddock countered. "I've read about Scott's expedition and I remember what happened with Grace. His body wasn't found by the search parties who went looking for Scott, and that was a hundred years ago. Not only is he probably buried under fifty feet of ice, but the ice itself is constantly moving, so even if you had the exact coordinates where he died—which you don't—he wouldn't be there."

Kismet nodded. "I've retained the services of a top-notch engineering firm to help me locate and recover Garral's body. Their expert puts the ice cover closer to seventy-five feet and he estimates the ice has advanced about thirty miles closer to the Ross Sea. That gave us a ballpark to play in. After that, we plugged in survey data from Operation IceBridge to identify anomalous densities in the target zone at the estimated depth."

Operation IceBridge, Kismet explained, was a NASA program designed to produce a comprehensive database of polar ice in order to accurately gauge the effects of climate change. Survey aircraft equipped with an extensive array of remote sensing technologies made repeated flights over the ice sheets, building a detailed three-dimensional model that went all the way down to bedrock—as deep as two miles in some places—or to the sea, as was the case with the Ross Ice shelf.

Maddock was impressed, and a little jealous of the resources Kismet had at his disposal. "Your guy found something?"

Kismet shrugged. "A few somethings. Unfortunately, the radar can only tell us where the anomalies are, not what they are."

"So it might be a body," Bones muttered, "or it might just be a big pile of penguin crap."

"I'm afraid so," Kismet admitted. "We've identified more than a dozen anomalies and prioritized them based on location and size. Our best match has an 86% probability, but there's only one way to know for sure."

Bones rolled his eyes. "If it's anything like ice-fishing, count me out. Unless there's a lot of beer, that is."

"Sounds time-consuming," Maddock said. "And with Prometheus breathing down our necks, time is one thing we don't have a lot of."

"You're right," Kismet said. "If they haven't figured out where you went or that you're with me, they soon will. We'll probably only get one shot at this."

There was a lurch as Ivan came to a full stop in front of the reception building.

"You can chill here…" Kismet started to say, then stopped himself. "Uh, I mean stay here. Arrange your own transportation home. Or you can head to the work site with me. It's a couple hours by helicopter. Honestly, I don't know what the safest option is."

"I think we're all in this together," Maddock said, then glanced at Bones and Rose. The latter nodded. Bones glowered, but didn't contradict his partner, or even offer one of his typically off-color wisecracks. Maddock took that as a vote in favor.

10

After a brief stopover in the sprawling quasi-city that was McMurdo Station they headed to the helicopter operations center to board a waiting Bell 212 for the flight to the work site. When Kismet had mentioned an engineering firm, Maddock had expected to find a small army of roughnecks deploying industrial equipment and derricks to support vertical drills, but as they approached, all he saw was a bright yellow festival-sized tent, looking forlorn in the bleak white landscape, about two hundred yards from the designated landing pad. As the helicopter touched down, a figure in a heavy parka emerged from the tent, and pulled back a flap closure to permit a tracked vehicle, fitted with a large fuel tank, to roll out into the open. The man in the parka swung up into the cab of the refuel vehicle, after which it surged forward to meet the helicopter.

While the driver of the fuel truck set about the task of topping off the Bell's tanks, the passenger came over to meet Kismet and the others. He threw back his hood to reveal a full head of dark, shoulder length hair and a young but craggy, deeply tanned visage, partially hidden behind a pair of mirrored aviator-style sunglasses. "Didn't expect you back so soon," the man said, gripping Kismet's hand.

"Things happened fast," Kismet said, then turned to make the introductions. "Jason Quinn, this is Maddock, Rose and… uh, Bones. Jason is a senior project director at ARGO."

Maddock was familiar with ARGO—the acronym stood for Alpine Research and Geographical Observation. The Colorado-based enterprise, originally established in 1902 by President Teddy Roosevelt as a scientific agency tasked with exploration and development in cold-weather climates, had eventually gone private, transforming into one of the world's leading civil engineering services, though they continued to work closely with the US government.

Quinn shook hands with the new arrivals one by one, but when he exchanged clasps with Bones, one of his eyebrows came up from behind a mirror lens and he grinned mischievously. "Bones, huh? And here I thought we were looking for a fully intact cadaver."

"On that subject," Kismet said. "Any progress?"

"Please say you found the frozen stiff and we can all go home," Bones said, hopefully.

The man grinned. "Come and see for yourself."

He led them on foot back to the tent. Under the voluminous yellow canopy, surrounded by huge piles of what looked like fresh powder snow, was a nine-foot wide hole, its depths hidden in shadow.

Bones' crack about ice-fishing wasn't far off the mark, but it was ice fishing with a high-tech upgrade.

Sitting alongside the hole was a strange-looking machine that looked like a cross between a robotic octopus and the shredder disc from the world's biggest Cuisinart.

"That's our baby," Quinn said, pointing to the device. "We call it the Ice Worm. It's an autonomous ice borer, equipped with radar and M-wave sensors."

Maddock thought he detected a hint of pride in Quinn's tone; it was the same pride he heard in Bones' voice whenever he employed their remote underwater vehicle, which he lovingly nicknamed Uma.

"The cutter head is studded with diamond blades," Quinn went on. "Diamond is just about the best conductor of heat, which means the cutter can turn at high RPMs without melting the ice and turning this place into a slushy nightmare. The manipulator arms are just there to hold it in place. All this…" He gestured to the mounds of snow piled up around them. "Is shaved ice—about 4,700 cubic feet worth. We use blower fans to create a negative air-pressure environment in here. Sucks the ice right out of the shaft."

"You make it sound easy," Maddock remarked.

Quinn shrugged. "There's a lot to be said for having the right tools for the job. Unfortunately, the Ice Worm can only get us to within about six inches of the target anomaly. Any deeper, and we run the risk of accidentally shredding the target." He walked over to a table near the machine and bent over a waiting laptop computer. "Take a look."

A couple mouse clicks woke the computer up

and a couple more brought up a grainy monochrome image. It didn't take much imagination to see the shape of a human body, curled up as if in repose. "I think that's our guy," Quinn announced. "But you'll have to do the rest the hard way."

"Ice fishing," groaned Bones.

"'Fraid so," Quinn said. "As soon as Curtis gets done fueling the helo, we'll start rigging the lines so you can go down." He paused a beat. "I expect you'll want to handle the recovery personally."

Kismet nodded.

"I'll go down with you," Maddock said. "Two can work faster than one." At a questioning glance from Kismet, he added, "Might as well make myself useful. What else is there to do?"

Alleviating boredom was only part of the reason why Maddock had volunteered to go into the pit. The truth of it was that Kismet's search had fired his own curiosity.

He expected to be challenged by the other members of the party. Expected to hear Jade demanding to go in his place since she had provided the clue that had brought Kismet here. Expected to hear Bones claim that *he* was the better climber. Expected Quinn to pull rank or cite some made-up safety concern.

But no one spoke up. Jade stared at him, blankly. Quinn shrugged. Bones just muttered, "Well I sure as hell ain't crawlin' into that frozen ice hole."

Kismet simply nodded. "Thanks."

Maddock gave Jade a meaningful glance then nodded toward Bones. "You two… Don't kill each other, okay?"

Jade frowned. "Don't look at me."

Maddock knew better than to ask for more, but doubted there would be any problems. The friction between his ex-girlfriend and his best friend was like the fire triangle; remove one corner from the equations—namely himself—and there would be no flames.

He turned to Rose. "One other thing…"

11

Maddock, a more experienced climber than Kismet, went first, rappelling into the borehole. Under normal circumstances, fast-roping down without a belayer would have posed no challenge to either of them, but the frigid temperatures and the requisite protective equipment brought with it a whole new set of variables. Maddock made a cautious descent, using the points of the crampons strapped to his mountaineering boots for traction, as he methodically worked his way down the smooth curving wall of the shaft. The blue-white interior of the borehole reflected and amplified the beam from his headlamp, lighting up the confined space like the old ice tunnel ride at Universal Studios. Finally, after about five tedious minutes of down climbing, he reached the bottom.

The floor of the shaft bore the marks of the Ice Worm's teeth, a pattern of concentric grooves radiating from the center, under a scattering of ice powder, but beneath the scoured translucent surface, Maddock could easily distinguish a large dark mass, pressed up against it like an insect trapped in amber. He looked away, turning his attention to the immediate task, and called up. "I'm set." His voice echoed weirdly.

After a few seconds, Kismet's voice, distant and distorted, came back. "On belay?"

Maddock held the twinned ropes in his gloved

hands, ready to take up the slack in the unlikely event Kismet lost control of his descent, and shouted back, "Belay on."

"Descending!"

The rope twitched in Maddock's grip as the other man made a careful but rapid descent without incident, and ninety seconds later, Kismet was standing beside him.

"So much for the easy part," Kismet remarked, staring back up the long shaft.

Maddock nodded his agreement. Getting back to the surface would be a test of both skill and endurance. They would have to front-point their crampons into the ice and inch their way back up the rope using mechanical ascenders, but that ordeal was the last thing on Maddock's mind. As Kismet began sweeping away the powdery ice shavings, Maddock unslung the backpack he'd brought down, and took out the black orb they had recovered from the Outpost and set it down on the floor, directly above the dark shape under the ice.

The orb was about eighteen inches or so in diameter, but unusually light, like a piece of Styrofoam. When they had first discovered it at the bottom of what might or might not have been a man-made pyramid hidden under the ice, it had actually been floating a few feet off the ground, suspended in some kind of invisible force field. That same force field had sublimated the ice surrounding it, turning it from a solid into a vapor without first melting it into water and without producing any detectable heat. Maddock was hoping to make it repeat that trick now, but after a minute or so of rolling it back and forth, there was no detectable change.

He looked up at Kismet and shrugged. "Well, it seemed like a good idea at the time."

"Maybe there's a step you missed," Kismet said. "How did you get it to work back at the Outpost?"

"I don't think we did anything. It just sort of woke up all on its own." Even as he said it, he realized that wasn't quite accurate. They had done something, albeit not intentionally. "The tomahawk," he said, thinking aloud.

The sunken wreckage of the seaplane had not been the only clue to lead Maddock and the others to the Outpost. They had also found a metal hatchet head, engraved with the name of a pre-Revolutionary War soldier named Stephen Thorne. The strange history of that artifact had brought them together with Rose Greer, who had supplied the missing pieces of the puzzle, but the tomahawk had done something else, too. The blade, infused with a rare metal Rose had identified as 'adamantine' had been drawn to the orb like a magnet. Before taking the orb down into the borehole, Maddock had peeled the hatchet head away and entrusted it to Rose for safe-keeping, but now he wondered if perhaps the two objects worked together to create the phenomena he had earlier observed. Before he could explain this to Kismet however, the other man began stripping off his gloves.

"I've got an idea."

Maddock sucked in an apprehensive breath. Although the bottom of the borehole was considerably warmer than the air outside the tent, sheltered and insulated by the ice itself, like the inside of an igloo, the temperature was still well below freezing. Without the protection of his gloves, Kismet would experience frostbite in a matter of minutes. The other man seemed unconcerned however. He flexed his fingers and rubbed them together for a moment, then reached up to his neck and unfastened the collar of his heavy winter parka.

Maddock caught a glimpse of something, a block of gleaming blue stone worn like a pendant around Kismet's neck, and knew it had to be the Apex stone Jade and Kismet had talked about, the talisman that had prompted Kismet's search for John Edward Grace. Kismet closed his left fist around the Apex, and then reached out and placed his right hand on the orb.

At first, Maddock didn't think anything was happening. There was no pyrotechnic display, no discharge of electricity. But after a few seconds, he realized that the air around them was growing thick with fog. He swept his hand through the mist, trying to brush it away, but like smoke, the vapors were pulled into the vacuum created by the movement, but in that brief moment, he saw clearly the results of Kismet's experiment.

The ice was giving up its dead.

Kismet remained like that for a full two minutes before drawing his hand back away from the orb. His bare fingers were covered in a dusting of ice crystals, but he shook them off and then stuffed his hands back into his gloves. The mist began dissipating immediately, coalescing into snowflakes which settled onto the floor, still partly obscuring what the orb had revealed. Kismet brushed the snow away to reveal the body, now completely free from its frozen tomb.

The cadaver lay on its side in a fetal curl, a last futile attempt to preserve body heat. Kismet gently rolled him over. In the stillness, the sound of the still frozen body crunching on the snow was both surreal and ominous. Then Maddock got a look at the man's face.

He couldn't recall if he'd ever seen a picture of the explorer, but making the identification would have been easy for anyone who had. The face peering up from the fur-lined hood had a leathery yellow cast, except around the nose which was shriveled and black, and the man's lips had pulled back to form a wide grimace, but otherwise the body was almost perfectly preserved, even the eyes which were open in an eternal sightless stare.

"Is it him?" he asked. "Grace?"

Kismet nodded but said nothing. After a moment of silent regard, he reached out and began peeling back the stiff fur garments. He rooted around for a while and then drew out a rectangular parcel that might have been a leather pouch or book cover. As Kismet meticulously unwrapped it, allowing it to fall open in his hands, Maddock saw that it was the latter.

The cold arid environment had left the paper brittle but the writing was crisp and legible.

"His diary," Kismet said, cautiously turning the pages, only giving each a brief glance. "I think we may have solved another mystery," he said after a reading a few pages. "I think the reason he decided to leave the others was to make sure nobody ever found this."

"A secret worth dying for?" Maddock said.

"Bigger than that. This would have outed him, and not just as an occult practitioner if you get my meaning."

Maddock was pretty sure he did.

"He knew he was going to die," Kismet went on, "and he knew that if this record ever made it back to civilization, his legacy as a heroic explorer would be tainted by—"

He broke off as something slid out of the book, fluttering as it fell, and came to rest on the cadaver's chest.

It was a stiff piece of paper, like a card or bookmark, adorned with an elaborate painted image. Maddock's first thought was that the object was a picture postcard, but the proportions weren't quite right; the card was narrow and oblong, more like an over-sized playing card. Kismet retrieved the card and held it up for closer inspection.

The picture was of a smiling nude figure. The

subject was androgynous, but seemed more male than female. Rising up behind him was a familiar representation of a caduceus—a staff with wings and two entwined snakes, often used—mistakenly— as a symbol of medicine. The figure's face was turned up, as if gazing at the sun, and his arms were outstretched, one raised higher than the other, and hanging in the air around him, like falling objects caught in a freeze frame were several strange objects adorned with cryptic symbols; Maddock didn't recognize them but felt like he should. There were other esoteric designs on the painting and a strange web of lines, like cables on a suspension bridge, radiated out from behind the figure. The man's feet were crossed, left over right, as if he was being crucified on the caduceus, but something that looked almost like another pair of wings spread out from his heels, covering the lower half of the painting.

"It's Hermes," Maddock said. "Or Mercury, but they're more or less the same. See the winged sandals and the caduceus?"

Kismet nodded in agreement, then flipped the card over to reveal another image, a cross that divided into multi-colored panels, and at its center, a single red rose.

Kismet gave a thoughtful hum. "The Rose Cross. It's one of the oldest symbols of alchemy." He looked up at Maddock. "This is a tarot card."

Maddock didn't know much about occult practices so he took Kismet at his word. "So it's not the map?"

Kismet turned the card back to the image of Hermes. "I think maybe it is. Look at these symbols.

"There are four suits in the Tarot deck, just like regular playing cards. Each one is linked to one of the four elements of esoteric tradition—fire, earth, water, and air." He pointed to the object close to the god's right hand. It reminded Maddock of the Olympic torch, except entwined with the flames was an equilateral triangle. "This represents the suit of staffs or wands—or clubs. It corresponds to the element of fire. And this shape here—the triangle—that's a fire symbol. Only I don't think it's just a triangle. It's a pyramid."

"That makes sense," Maddock agreed. "The word pyramid comes from an ancient Greek term that translates as 'fire in the middle.' So that's one. What about spades, hearts and diamonds?"

"In tarot, the suits are wands, swords, cups and coins—also called disks or pentacles." He chuckled. "I really fell down the rabbit hole doing research on Adam Garral. Anyway, this black object below it definitely looks like a disk to me. And this…" His gloved fingertip shifted over to Hermes' left side, to an object that resembled a trophy or two-handed drinking cup. Directly above it was another circle, but unlike the disk, it was rendered in such a way as to suggest a three-dimensional shape—a sphere.

"Cups," Maddock said, catching on. "Water."

Kismet nodded. "Modernized into the suit of hearts. Hearts pump blood which is mostly water.

This last one…" He slid his finger down to the final image which appeared to be a puffy cloud pierced by something that looked like a shard of glass or a jagged lightning bolt. "That must be swords, representing the element of air."

"Okay. I'll buy that it's a tarot card, but how is it a map?"

"I'm not sure it's a literal map, although it might be. It's more like a set of instructions for a scavenger hunt. Adam Garral found one piece of the puzzle in Egypt, in the Great Pyramid."

"The Apex."

"He was down here looking for another."

"Which one?" Even as he asked it, Maddock realized the answer. "The orb. That's what he was looking for. But which one is it?"

"If I had to guess, I'd say cups. The shape, like a drop of water. And it was sealed up in ice."

Maddock recalled how Kismet had used the Apex and the orb in concert to evaporate the ice covering the frozen remains of John Edward Grace. "So now we have two pieces. What do we win if we collect all four?"

"Immortality. The ability to transmute the elements." Kismet nodded toward the corpse on the floor. "That's what he thought anyway."

"And Prometheus? What do they want with it."

"What else? Power."

"Everybody wants to rule the world," Maddock muttered. "So I guess we better find the other two pieces first, and make sure they don't get their hands on any of them."

Kismet laughed softly. "I like the way you think, Dane Maddock."

"It's Bones. He's a bad influence. So, any idea where to look next?"

"One or two." Kismet dropped the card back into the journal then closed the leather cover and stuffed the parcel into the pocket of his parka. "But first, let's go somewhere warmer. I think we've accomplished all we can down here."

Maddock knew he wasn't just talking about the borehole. "Bones will be glad to hear it."

Kismet stood and moved back, giving Maddock room to retrieve the orb. When the black sphere was again nestled in the backpack slung over Maddock's shoulder, Kismet knelt beside the remains of the polar explorer and leaned in close. "Don't worry, old man," he whispered. "Your secret's safe forever."

12

Because air transport was a scarce resource in Antarctica, the helicopter that had brought them to the work site had returned to McMurdo Station, and wouldn't be available again for several hours. So while Quinn and his partner Curtis Johnson—a gregarious fellow with a grin as big as a Halloween jack-o-lantern—began bulldozing the ice shavings into the borehole, both to rebury Grace and at least partially return the landscape to its original condition, Kismet, following Rose's advice, went to work creating digital copies of both the journal and the strange tarot card.

Rose had immediately recognized the image on the card, confirming and clarifying Kismet's original identification.

"This is the Magus card from the Thoth deck created by Aleister Crowley," she said, enlarging the image on the screen of Kismet's tablet computer. "A version of it, anyway. There are some differences."

"Thoth was an Egyptian god, right?" Maddock said.

Rose nodded. "The god of wisdom and knowledge."

"Isn't Thoth also the Egyptian version of Hermes?"

"The ancients made that connection, though strictly speaking, the god on this card is a representation of Mercury."

"Same dif," Bones muttered.

"There are similarities, but they aren't the same," Rose insisted. "Crowley was very particular about the imagery he chose for this deck, and specifically this card. He wasn't happy with the first few attempts, much to the chagrin of his collaborator, Lady Frieda Harris. He made her paint at least four different versions before finally settling on one that looked pretty much like this. He didn't call it the Magus, though. His name for the card was the Juggler, which is more consistent with the symbolism used in earlier decks, where the magician isn't a sorcerer but more of a sleight-of-hand performer. His decision to show a divine figure instead of a human was very controversial among occultists of his time." She paused a beat and then delivered her caveat. "John Edward Grace disappeared in 1912. Crowley didn't start work on his tarot deck until 1938."

"How is that possible?" Jade asked.

Bones shrugged. "Duh. Magic."

Kismet stared at the image on the screen with renewed interest. "You said this isn't exactly the same as Crowley's card."

"If we had WiFi down here, I'd show you a side-by-side comparison."

"Is it possible that Crowley and Grace knew each other?"

"Assuming that he and Adam Garral are one and the same, I'd say it's very likely. They traveled in the same circles, and I don't just mean the occult.

Crowley was a renowned mountaineer and world traveler. It's also widely believed that he was working for British intelligence. That story you told us about Garral spending a night in the Great Pyramid. Crowley claimed to have done that also. Maybe they both did, or maybe he borrowed the story from Garral. Either way, I don't think it's a coincidence."

Maddock saw where things were headed. "So maybe Garral-slash-Grace showed Crowley this card back in 19-aught-whatever, and thirty years later, Crowley tried to reproduce it from memory."

"I still say magic," Bones said. "But if the egg came before the chicken, where did iceman get the card in the first place?"

"Hand painted tarot decks have been around since the 15th Century. They would have been collector's items for occult enthusiasts in the 19th and early 20th. But like I said, the imagery on the Thoth Magus is unique."

"Whoever painted this one knew about the Apex. And the orb from the Outpost."

"John Dee!" Jade exclaimed.

"It's pronounced: 'Yahtzee,'" Bones said.

Jade ignored him. "Grace must have found the card in the Liber whatchamacallit, the same way you found it in his diary."

Kismet inclined his head toward her. "That makes sense. And if Dee really was some kind of seer, maybe he saw the Apex and the orb in one of his visions."

"Dee didn't have visions," Jade corrected. "Kelly was the one who had the visions. Dee just wrote it all down." When she realized everyone was looking at her expectantly, she grimaced. "I heard that somewhere. But the point is, he saw them." She turned to Kismet. "Remember how the manuscript talked about the elemental temples? Pyramids! Your great-grandfather found the Apex in the Great Pyramid in Egypt. Maddock found the orb in a pyramid under the ice."

"So the other two are also in pyramids," Maddock said. "Where?"

Jade shook her head. "No. Dee already had one piece. The smoking mirror from the temple of Tezcatlipoca. An Aztec pyramid!"

"Obsidian," Kismet mused. "That would represent the earth element."

"And it's shaped like a disk," Jade added.

Bones wagged his head. "Does anybody else think this is...you know, a reach? We've got an Aztec artifact that's probably... what, a few hundred years old. Then we've got something from an Egyptian pyramid that could be five thousand years old. And that orb...who even knows who put it there? And yet somehow, this kooky old mystic saw it all."

Ten years earlier, Maddock would have agreed wholeheartedly, but now he wasn't so quick to dismiss the seemingly impossible. "It's not the strangest thing we've seen," he said, and then, with a wry smile added. "Could be aliens, traveling in time and space."

Bones' skepticism immediately vanished as he latched on to the suggestion. "Aliens. Of course."

"Dee's mirror," Kismet said. "It's in the British Museum. I've seen it. And I'd be willing to bet Adam Garral saw it, too. It led him to the Apex stone, and then it led him here." He raised his eyes to the others. "There's just one piece left. Air. The sword. But where?"

Bones stroked his chin in mock-thoughtfulness. "I'm thinking it's in a pyramid. Rose? What do you think?"

She shrugged. "Don't look at me. I've read a couple books on Crowley, but I'm no expert on this occult stuff."

Jade offered a cryptic grin. "I think we need to look in the mirror."

13

Bones tilted his head back and stared up at the elaborately sculpted façade fronting the British Museum. "Have we been here before? I feel like we've been here before."

Maddock searched his memory, then shrugged. "With all our adventures, it's hard to keep track."

"No kidding. And don't even get me started on alternate timelines."

Jade wagged her head in mock despair. "Is that supposed to be funny, Bonebrake? 'Cause if so, you should go back to what you're best at—fourth-grade potty jokes."

Bones nodded as if he had just scored major points. "So you admit it. I am the best."

Kismet leaned close to Rose and in a stage whisper, asked, "Remind me again; which one did she used to date?"

Jade just rolled her eyes and headed inside.

Maddock allowed himself a chuckle. Despite two exhausting days of travel, they were all in good spirits, a fact that probably had something to do with the weather. Despite being a gray and drizzly 45° Fahrenheit, London might have been Key West after the sub-zero temperatures they had endured in Antarctica.

Jade led the way inside and went to the

reception desk to check in. A few minutes later, a petite woman with cinnamon-colored hair called out to her from across the lobby. "Jade! Great to see you again!"

"Kelly!" Jade met the woman halfway, offering her hand only to get caught in an awkward hug. "Come on. Let me introduce the others."

"Others?" Allenby said, with an impish grin. "So this isn't a solo adventure?"

"Not this time," Jade said with a grin.

As Maddock shook Allenby's hand, he had a strange moment of déjà vu, as if she was already an old friend. He chalked it up to the reality bending properties of the elemental relics. With the introductions out of the way, Allenby led them to her office where the piece they had traveled halfway around the world to see sat innocuously on her desktop alongside her laptop computer.

Maddock sucked in an apprehensive breath as he laid eyes on it, and sensed a similar reaction from the others. Jade—the only one of their group who had not witnessed some kind of phenomena associated with either the orb or the Apex stone— stared at the others for a moment and then approached the obsidian mirror.

The relic was about six-inches in diameter and shaped like a teardrop, with a hole drilled through a tab-like extension on the narrow end, as if it was meant to be hung from a nail or worn like a necklace. The hard volcanic glass did provide a reflection like a mirror, but considerably darkened.

After what seemed like a few minutes, Jade said, "Well? Anything?"

Maddock glanced over at Kismet. The latter was gripping the Apex stone in his left fist, as if trying to summon its power. After a moment, he reached out with his right hand and touched the mirror, but nothing happened.

"Should we try the orb?" Rose suggested, giving her backpack a meaningful shake.

Kismet shook his head. "I don't think it would do any good. This isn't the right mirror."

"A fake?"

"Not necessarily," Allenby said from behind them. She wore a slightly perplexed expression, as if not quite sure why her visitors had been so quick to dismiss the artifact as less than genuine. "As I've told Jade, the provenance for the Dee pieces in our collection was never solidly established. We have only the word of Horace Walpole that it ever belonged to Dee, but it is an Aztec mirror. There is no question about that. Walpole received it from Lord Frederick Campbell in 1771, and claimed it had been Dee's scrying glass. That would have been more than a century and a half after Dee's death, and there's no mention of it anywhere during the intervening time period." She smiled then, as if laughing at a private joke. "Walpole *was* a novelist, so he might have made the whole thing up. They do that sometimes, you know."

Bones let out a groan of dismay.

They had all earlier discussed the possibility—the likelihood even—that the mirror in the British Museum might not be the smoking mirror described in the Dee manuscript, and what it would mean for their search if that proved to be the case, but Maddock wasn't ready to throw in the towel just yet. "When did the museum acquire this mirror?"

"I believe it was in 1966," Allenby said.

"Half a century after Adam Garral's disappearance," Kismet said. They had all agreed not to bring up the name John Edward Grace.

"Where was it in between? From 1771 to 1966? Specifically, where was it in the early 1900s?"

Allenby circled around her desk and opened her laptop. After a few keystrokes, she began reading aloud. "In 1906 it was put up for auction at Sotheby's, part of the Collection of Hollingworth Magniac, but withdrawn. Hmm. Magniac was a collector of medieval art. He died in 1867 but his son Charles maintained the collection until his death in 1891. No mention of it until the Museum acquired it from Rev. R.W. Stannard in 1966. I'll have to do some more digging to uncover how it came into his possession."

Maddock turned back to the others. "Doesn't sound like this particular mirror was making the rounds in the occult movement."

"Mirrors like this aren't exactly rare," Allenby said. "To the best of my knowledge, this is the only one actually linked to Dr. John Dee, but who's to say if that's really the case."

"And the others? Where would we start looking?"

"A year ago, I would have told you to go visit Gerald Roche. If it's not in a private collection, something like that would probably end up at the Museum of Magick in Plymouth." She rolled her eyes as she said it. "Magic spelled with a 'k'."

Bones screwed up his face in an expression of mock-confusion. "K-A-G-I-C?"

"That's a real thing?" Maddock asked, ignoring his partner. "Sounds like a tourist trap."

"They must be doing something right, because they're surprisingly well funded." Allenby looked over at Jade. "Most of the manuscripts from Roche's collection ended up there."

"If Garral's copy of the *Liber Loagaeth* went there," Jade said, "maybe the mirror did, too."

Maddock was thinking the same thing, but made an effort to temper his enthusiasm. "It's a place to start looking."

14

Plymouth, England

The Museum of Magick—with a 'k'—occupied an old stone building that looked like it might once have been a fortress or a church. The structure appeared to have been built into the side of the limestone cliff, and had a commanding view of the Plymouth Sound, where the Mayflower had begun its famous voyage, bearing the pilgrims to the New World. Not surprisingly, the area was brimming with tourist attractions, including a world-class aquarium, a historic royal citadel, an art deco public pool, and a seventy-foot-tall red and white lighthouse, which had once stood nine miles out to sea on the treacherous reef known as the Eddystone Rocks. As was the case with most seaside tourist destinations, there was little activity given the season and the blustery weather, but the shops and attractions were still open for business, including the Museum of Magick.

Plymouth was three-and-a-half hours from London by train, and nearly six by car, so they chose the former, catching a taxi from the station to the Museum's front door. Braving the rain, they hurried inside and approached the ticket counter where a young man with shoulder-length wavy blond hair, dressed all in black, greeted them with an amused if slightly surprised smile which brightened a few degrees when he saw Rose and Jade.

"Thought I was going to be able to shutter early," the young man said. "Guess it's a good thing I didn't."

"Must be our lucky day," Bones muttered.

They paid the entry fee, a modest £5 apiece, and headed directly inside, browsing the exhibits which were, contrary to Maddock's expectations, more informative than sensational. The displays began in pre-Roman times with the Druids and other pagan religions, which laid the foundation for Wicca and other modern traditions of witchcraft, then moved into the history of religious persecution of witches, to include those who were guilty of nothing more than using herbs and other traditional healing methods. At one point, Bones launched into an impromptu performance of the "witch-test" scene from Monty Python and the Holy Grail.

"So if she weighs the same as a duck," he said in terrible approximation of a British accent, pointing at Jade, who returned a withering scowl. "Then she's made of wood."

"And therefore?" said a voice from behind them with a far more convincing accent.

Everyone turned to see the young man who had taken their money at the door, entering the gallery.

"A witch!" Bones chortled.

Jade shot daggers at him. "Maybe I should turn you into a newt. Oh, wait. That would be an improvement."

"We like witches here," the young man said, beaming at Jade.

Jade managed a half-hearted smile. "I'm not a witch. But thanks."

"A goddess then," he said with a wink.

Bones gave a disgusted snort, but Maddock, sensing that Jade might be able to make use of the attention she was receiving, shot an elbow into his friend's ribs. Bones grunted, but didn't say anything more.

Message received.

"Since we're a bit slow at the moment," the young man continued, "I thought I'd check up on you lot. I'm Aramis." He stuck out his hand. "Aramis Black."

Maddock pre-emptively elbowed Bones again.

Jade shook the proffered hand and quickly introduced everyone, first names only.

"If you have any questions," Black said, "I'll do my best to answer."

"Actually," Jade said, "We heard you had one of the best collections of Dee manuscripts. We were hoping to get a look at some of those."

Black registered pleasant surprise again. "I see you didn't just come here on a lark. Yes, that's correct. We have an entire room devoted to Dee. He was the first to truly bridge the gap between the spirit realm and scientific understanding. His work is the foundation for our exploration of magic."

"Is that magic with a 'k'?" Bones asked.

Black seemed not to hear. "The Dee Room is

just ahead, but I'm afraid the manuscripts you're asking about aren't on display. They're reserved for scholars."

"We *are* scholars," Jade said, then nodded toward Bones. "Except for him. He's just a cretin. I'm an archaeologist. Rose here is a history professor. Our interest in the manuscripts is academic."

"I should have chosen my words more carefully," the man said. "What I meant to say is that they are reserved for the initiated."

Sensing that the answer would test Jade's patience, Maddock stepped forward. "Then this isn't just a museum. It's a temple, as well."

"In a manner of speaking."

"And I take it you're not just the guy that works the counter."

"No. I am an adept, and among other things, I am the historian of the Order."

"We aren't initiates," Kismet said. "But my great-grandfather was. Adam Garral."

Black raised a skeptical eyebrow. "Adam Garral was your great-grandfather?"

"Great-great actually, but yes. You've heard of him?"

"He was a great magician. One of the greatest. If he had not disappeared…" Black shook his head as if the century-old mystery was still a source of grief. "He was one of the founders. A pillar of the movement. Crowley took all the credit, but Garral was the wellspring. The true Therion. Some say he transcended this reality."

"I know that he was studying the *Liber Loagaeth* before his disappearance. I'm trying to retrace his footsteps, so to speak. Solve an old family mystery." Sensing he was on the right track, Kismet drew out the leather-bound journal and opened it, displaying the brightly-colored tarot card. "And maybe learn a little more about this."

The young man's eyes went wide as saucers.

Bones chuckled. "Not bad for a bunch of non-initiates."

Black looked up from the card, staring at Kismet with a mixture of awe and dread. "Where did you find this?"

Kismet held the journal up. "Family papers."

Black brought his fingertips together in what was either a thoughtful gesture or an attempt to enchant them. "Those would be a valuable addition to our collection. Perhaps we can come to some sort of arrangement."

Kismet appeared to consider the offer. "The papers are private, but I might be willing to make an indefinite loan of this card. Tell you what. We really came here looking for Dr. Dee's obsidian mirror."

"Dee's Speculum is in the British Museum in London," Black replied, a little too quickly.

"We've seen it. And I think we both know it's not the real deal."

"We have other mirrors in the collection," said

Black, equivocally. "I don't believe any are historically linked to Dr. Dee. You're welcome to have a look at them but if you're proposing an exchange… Well, I couldn't possibly authorize anything like that."

"Maybe we should be talking to someone else," Jade suggested.

Black frowned but then inclined his head. "You're right, of course. I'll ring the director straightaway. Why don't you continue your tour? There are several scrying mirrors in the spiritualist collection, just past the Dee room." He seemed about to add something more, but then changed his mind and simply exited without another word.

When he was gone, Bones let out a snort of laughter. "Aramis Black? Seriously?"

"I feel like we've already had this conversation," Jade said.

Bones shrugged. "Fair enough. Anyway, I'd love to play poker against him."

Maddock nodded. "He definitely knows something about the mirror. Did you notice how he reacted when you mentioned Adam Garral?"

Kismet gave a thoughtful nod. "I did. And I agree that he's not telling us everything. But it's his move."

They continued making their way through the exhibits. The Dee Room was a veritable shrine to the occult scholar. The walls were covered with photo-enlargements of pages from the Liber Loagaeth and other examples of Enochian writing, and there were a number of replica artifacts and a few that purported to be authentic. There was even a diorama of Dee and Kelley, sitting together, the former bent over an open book, writing, while the latter peered into a small crystal globe positioned above the distinctive magical diagram known as the *Sigillum Dei Aemaeth*—the symbol of the Living God—a seven-pointed star surrounding a five-pointed star, both inscribed with the names of God and several angels.

After the Dee Room came an exhibit chronicling the persecution of witches, both in England and in the American colonies. They didn't linger there, but pushed on to the exhibits concerned with the emergence of spiritualism and the occult in the late 19th and early 20th Century. Maddock was surprised to learn that both arose from serious, albeit misguided, scientific inquiry into the nature of both the universe and the human psyche. As with Dee, a Christian who believed he was in communication with angels, much of the belief system of both the spiritualists and the occultists—men like Aleister Crowley—derived from traditional religious belief systems—Christianity and Jewish mysticism. One display gave the story behind the unusual spelling of 'magick.' Crowley had added the extra letter to differentiate what he called, "the Science and Art of causing Change to occur in conformity with Will" from sleight of hand performance magic.

It was, Maddock thought, both fascinating and a little disconcerting. Those who believed in Crowley's system of Magick—also called Thelema—did so with a feverish intensity, enacting rituals that ranged from absurd to disturbing. Of course, the same could be said for the rites of most religions. What was the Eucharist if not a sympathetic ritual, eating God's flesh and blood in order to gain some special favor with the spirit realm. It was just human nature to desire power over life and death, and all religions represented a concerted effort to find it. Magick was no different.

And yet, Adam Garral had used occult knowledge to find the Apex. Had his magical studies allowed him to unlock real supernatural power? Or had he merely gotten lucky, stumbling over the discovery while looking for something else, mistaking coincidence for some sort of divine action?

Maddock did not share these musings with the others. He wasn't as interested in understanding the power of the elemental relics as he was in keeping them out of the wrong hands, and he sensed Kismet shared that mission.

Black returned, an eager smile on his youthful face. He moved in close, speaking in a conspiratorial whisper. "I couldn't tell you this before, but…" His eyes darted back and forth, a touch too dramatically. "I know why you've come. The mirror you seek… The Magna of Illusion. The first elemental. I will take you to it."

15

The gray sky had deepened by several shades during their brief tour of the museum, and Maddock knew that the full dark of night wasn't far off. A persistent drizzle that didn't quite qualify as rain continued to dampen the world, but the waves crashing against the nearby Mount Batten breakwater hinted at a storm yet to come. He studied the turbulent sea for a few seconds and then turned to appraise the boat that Black was preparing for launch. The 21-foot Zodiac Pro Open 650 rigid-hulled inflatable was an excellent platform for diving and other recreational and utilitarian activities, but not ideally suited for the current weather conditions.

"Maybe we should wait until morning," he said.

"Ordinarily, this is where I would make a comment about Maddock being a wuss," said Bones, hugging his arms close to his chest as if remembering the chill of Antarctica anew. They were all a little soggy from the short walk to the harbor, but that was nothing to the soaking they would get out on the water. "But just this once, I happen to agree with him."

Black did not look up from his task. "We only have to go a little ways," he said, and pointed out across the harbor to a land mass. "Drake's Island. Just there. It's only about half-a-mile. The weather is only going to get worse, so if we don't go now, we might have to wait days."

"Why there?" Jade asked.

"That's where the Magna of Illusion is kept. We have a…" He paused as if trying to find the appropriate word. "A secure facility there. A private place where initiates can practice without distraction." He clambered over the inflated pontoons, to the pilot's bolster situated amidships, donned an orange personal flotation collar, and then settled in behind the wheel. "I'll tell you all about it on the way."

Maddock exchanged a look with Bones, then with Kismet. Both men just shrugged. Of course, they were going; what choice did they have? Black was calling the shots and he did not seem inclined to postpone the journey. Moreover, he was right about the weather. As SEALs, Maddock and Bones had both conducted boat operations under less favorable conditions, using rigid-hulled inflatable boats nearly identical to Black's Zodiac.

When they were all aboard and wearing life preservers, Black started the outboard and cast off, motoring slowly away from the pier until he was in the channel route. Once he was in the clear, he increased the throttle until the Zodiac's V-shaped polyester hull was plowing through swells. Under sunnier skies, it would have been an exciting experience, but with the gray drizzle, it seemed merely like an ordeal to be endured.

The seas calmed a little as they approached the north side of the island, which faced back toward

Plymouth, but the sky continued to darken, prompting Black to bring out a flashlight to illuminate the way ahead. The crossing took about ten minutes, during which time Black told them a little about their destination.

Named for the famed explorer and privateer, Sir Francis Drake, the island had historically served as a defensive gun emplacement to safeguard Plymouth Harbor until, following World War II, such measures were deemed unnecessary. The city had used the island, with its abandoned military barracks, as a boy's adventure camp for a while, but eventually it had been sold off to a developer who had never quite managed to develop anything there. Although Black didn't come right out and say it, Maddock got the impression the real estate developer was either an initiate in the occult movement, or at the very least, getting a pay-off to maintain the status quo.

"What was it you called the mirror?" Jade asked. "Something about an illusion?"

"The Magna of Illusion," Black said. Despite the fact that he was nearly yelling to be heard over the roar of the outboard, his tone was reverent. "Discovered by Geronimo de Aguilar and Gonzalo del Rio in the Pyramid of Tezcatlipoca in the Yucatan, in a chamber of jade, with only one way in and no way out. Captured by Sir Francis Drake and brought to England where Queen Elizabeth bestowed it to her astrologer, Dr. John Dee.

"Dee chose the name. It is a reference to St.

Paul's letter to the Corinthians: 'For now we see through a glass, darkly; but then face to face: now I know in part; but then shall I know even as also I am known.' In this mirror was revealed the word of angels, a vision of things to come and places unseen, but prophecy is only an illusion of what may come to pass, a possible future glimpsed in the dark glass."

The Zodiac drew up to the long pier jutting out from the island, Bones reached out with one long arm and caught the floating dock, steadying the boat while Maddock quickly tied the mooring line to a cleat. With the boat secure, they climbed out and followed Black up to the slick concrete pier.

At the end of the pier, they entered a stairwell passage cut into the cliffside. A short flight of moss-covered steps rose to a path that led them past dilapidated structures that had once housed and fed the artillerymen manning the island's defensive stations. Black led them through the midst of the abandoned complex without stopping, following the path as it curved back into the shadowy woods that dominated the crest of the island.

Rose caught up to Maddock as they left the barracks behind. "Maddock," she whispered. "I think we're close."

He nodded in acknowledgment, but then realized that she probably couldn't see the gesture. "I just hope this isn't another dead end."

"That's what I mean," she replied. "The orb. It's reacting to something. I can feel it moving in the pack. Shifting whenever we change directions, like a compass needle. I think it senses the mirror."

Maddock recalled how they had used the adamantine-infused tomahawk head like a dowsing rod to find the orb in Antarctica.

"The Apex is doing the same thing," Kismet whispered. "I think we're definitely in the right place this time."

As if overhearing their conversation, Black announced. "It's just in here." He shone his light toward a squat concrete building which Maddock guessed was a bunker or shelter built beneath an old gun emplacement. There was no door in the doorway and no glass in the windows, but otherwise the structure appeared solid enough. Black went inside, his body briefly eclipsing the light as he passed through the doorway. Maddock and the others filed in after him.

The bare floor was littered with beer cans, food wrappers and old blankets—the detritus of urban explorers and thrill seekers looking for a place to party. Black ignored the evidence of trespassers, and moved to the far wall to stand before a metal door with peeling yellow paint. The doorknob had been removed, leaving only the escutcheon. The door itself was secured with a rusty iron crossbar and serviceable padlock. The security measures might thwart vandals and trespassers, but it was hardly the level of security one would expect to safeguard a purportedly supernatural artifact.

Black produced a key and opened the lock, and then moved his hand to the missing door knob. He gave the escutcheon a twist, as if removing the lid from a jar of pickles, and it swiveled out of the way to reveal a small numerical keypad that looked anything but dilapidated. He punched in a code, and with a faint hiss of depressurization, the metal door began to move, swinging outward, and Maddock now saw that the door was actually just a façade hiding a heavy bank vault-type door.

Black darted inside the vault and reappeared a moment later with his flashlight tucked under one arm and a velvet-lined wooden box held reverently in both hands. Nestled inside the box was something that looked like a small, perfectly round window into another dimension. Even without the confirmation from the other elemental relics, Maddock would have known it was the real deal just by looking at it. Or into it.

Kismet seemed to know it as well. He met Black's gaze. "May I touch it?"

"Please do," Black said, his voice quavering in anticipation. "You are Adam Garral's heir. This should be quite spectacular."

Kismet reached out a tentative hand, touched the black mirror… And then drew back his hand as if he'd been shocked.

He looked over at Maddock and then the others. "Did you see…?" He let the question hang. Maddock hadn't seen anything unusual, but Kismet evidently had.

"What did *you* see?"

Kismet opened his mouth to answer, but then closed it again and shook his head. He turned to look at Black, who continued to regard him with a mixture of excitement and reverence.

"Kismet?" Maddock said, and then repeated the unanswered question. "What did you see?"

"I was somewhere else." He frowned. "Only I was here, too, at the same time. Everything was jumbled together."

"Amazing," Black said. "Most initiates must meditate for hours before the mirror reveals anything. And even then, it's rarely so vivid."

The Apex is giving him an assist, Maddock thought, but kept it to himself. No sense in volunteering that information to Black.

"Try again," Jade prompted.

Kismet nodded and did so, tilting his head forward to focus his gaze on the dark glass. His forehead creased in concentration. After a moment, he raised his head again and began looking around the abandoned bunker, but when he began speaking, it became apparent what he was seeing was not in the same reality.

"Pyramids," he whispered, turning a half-circle and craning his head around for a full 360° view. "Four of them. Jungle. Ice. Desert." He hesitated. "Sky."

Bones leaned close to Maddock and whispered, "A pyramid in the sky?" Maddock expected his friend to make a joke, but instead Bones took it a different direction. "Could be describing a UFO?"

"I've seen something like this before," Kismet went on. "I think it's the Tower of Babel."

Maddock got the reference immediately. According to the Bible book of Genesis, the descendants of Noah had come together to build a city and tower so high that it would reach the heavens. Their hubris had prompted God to intervene, disrupting the project before completion by confusing the languages of the builders, which caused them to scatter across the globe.

"Of course," Black said, his voice still full of awe. "You are seeing the elemental temples. The jungle temple. That would be the pyramid temple where the Magna of Illusion was found. A symbol of earth. The desert pyramid... Is it Egyptian?"

Kismet nodded slowly.

"Fascinating," Black went on. "That would certainly represent the element of fire. The Tower of Babel, a ziggurat meant to reach the heavens, would symbolize air. And ice? Well that can only signify water. I wonder where that one is?"

Maddock shot the others an urgent look, willing them all to keep silent about their discoveries.

Kismet continued turning his head, looking around at places and things only he could see. All of a sudden, he threw his arms out to the sides as if trying to regain his balance. His upper torso tilted back and forth for a few seconds before stabilizing. "Moving now. There are lines connecting the pyramids. Like wires or… A web? I'm moving along them. Jungle… Whoa!

"I'm inside now. It's disorienting. Like being in an Escher painting. The walls… Angles…" He trailed off for a moment then nodded. "The mirror. It's here. It was here. It was always here."

"Until it wasn't," Jade said.

Maddock nodded. "He's seeing the past."

Kismet swayed silently for several more seconds then lifted his hand away. "That's the real thing, all right." He gave Maddock a knowing look that said, *We got what we came for*, then met Black's gaze.

"Thank you." Kismet extended his right hand, offering the hand painted Magus card. "It's yours, as promised."

Black smiled, but there was neither humor nor gratitude in the expression. The indirect light rising from his flashlight gave him a ghoulish appearance. "You can't leave. Not yet."

Maddock experienced a shiver of apprehension, but then Black clarified his statement. "You've experienced a revelation. You must tell me what you beheld."

Kismet managed a patient smile of his own. "I already told you what I saw."

"I do not think you did," said another voice from behind them, a female voice that did not belong to Jade or Rose.

Maddock whirled to face the newcomer, an

exotic-looking raven-haired woman who gazed at them from the door to the bunker. Behind her stood several more figures; it was impossible to tell how many, but there were at least three, all male, all dressed in black. All holding guns.

"Aliyah," Jade said, hissing the name like a curse.

Maddock recognized the name from Jade's account of her initial meeting with Kismet. Aliyah Cerulean, the widow of Alexander Cerulean who had stolen the Apex from Kismet's father, and died in a fall from the Great Pyramid.

Aliyah took a step forward, entering the concrete bunker and clearing the doorway for the others, who immediately began swarming inside. Not three, but a dozen, all armed with pistols. Maddock and the others were surrounded in an instant, at least two guns trained on each of them. Everyone but Black who was still smiling.

Aliyah's eyes never left Kismet. "You haven't told us everything. But you will."

16

If the woman's sudden appearance surprised Kismet, he gave no indication, nor did he appear the least bit intimidated. "Poor Aliyah. Still trying to avenge your dead husband. I warned you what would happen."

Aliyah spat out a laugh like a bitter taste, then stepped closer. "You still think this is about revenge."

She reached for his throat but instead of strangling him, she tore at his collar, exposing the Apex hanging around his neck. She grasped it and then yanked it away hard enough to snap the string from which it hung.

Now Maddock understood. Aliyah was working with Black; she was probably part of his secret order of magicians, presumably the gunmen with her were also members. She was an initiate, perhaps even an adept—the word Black had used to describe himself. Her husband probably had been a senior member as well, which explained why he had stolen the Apex from Kismet's father.

Kismet inclined his head as if to concede her superior position. "I see. And now you have what you need to find the other elementals."

Aliyah did not deny it. With one hand still gripping the Apex, she turned and placed her other hand on the Magna of Illusion. She closed her eyes and remained that way for several seconds, then opened them again, unable to hide a look of disappointment.

"No reception?" Bones remarked.

Aliyah just stared at Kismet. "You know where they are. We all heard you. The four temples. Where are they? How are the elementals manifest in this world?"

When Kismet did not answer, she turned to one of her henchman—one of the men holding Jade at gunpoint—and nodded. Immediately, the man seized Jade's arm and spun her around so quickly she would have lost her balance if not for his grip. He pulled her close, stabbing the barrel of his gun into the tender flesh below her jaw.

Aliyah returned her attention to Kismet. "You will die," she said, matter-of-factly. "Honor demands it. But I have no quarrel with these others. How many of them will I have to kill to get you to cooperate? Just one?" She raised a hand, poised to deliver a chopping gesture, the signal to kill.

"No. Not even one," Kismet said in a quiet voice. "I'll tell you exactly what I saw." He glanced around, making eye contact with Black and several others. "I want your word. Swear by whatever gods you worship that you'll let them all go."

Maddock expected a contemptuous rejection, but to his astonishment, Aliyah simply nodded. "I swear it."

The promise did not ease Maddock's apprehension, but for the moment, there wasn't much he could do.

Kismet took a breath. "I saw four pyramids. You already know about two of them. The temple of Tezcatlipoca in Mexico. The Great Pyramid of Khufu in Egypt. The third temple was in a land of ice."

Aliyah let out a long hiss, the warning unmistakable.

"It's in Antarctica," Kismet said.

"Ah, so that is why you went there. Don't deny it. I know that you traveled there."

"I was there to find Adam Garral's remains. That's where I found the card and his journal. I didn't even know the rest of it until just now."

That was mostly true.

Aliyah's gaze narrowed suspiciously but after a moment she seemed to accept the logic of his answer. "Where exactly is it?"

"I'm afraid there weren't a lot of visible landmarks. I could probably find it with some help from Google."

"And the elemental? Did you see it?"

He nodded slowly, betraying nothing with his eyes. "It's a sphere. Some kind of strange black metal."

"And the fourth pyramid is the Tower of Babel?"

"I think so." He shook his head uncertainly, and Maddock sensed he was genuinely confused by whatever he had seen.

"I didn't even know that was a real thing," Bones muttered. Like Maddock, he seemed calm, unperturbable, but under the surface, poised to act.

"It was and it wasn't," Rose said. At first, her voice was a tremulous squeak, but then she straightened, as if drawing courage from the fact that they had already successfully hidden their possession of the orb from their tormentors. "There was a pyramid in Babylon, a ziggurat called the Etemenanki. It was a temple to the god Marduk. Many scholars believe it was the inspiration for the tower described in the Bible. The name literally means 'temple of the foundation of heaven and earth,' which is interesting because in the Bible, the builders' intent was to build a tower that reached the heavens. The book of Genesis says that the word 'Babel' means confusion, but it's more likely derived from *bab-el*—Gate of God."

Maddock gave her an encouraging nod. "Is it still there?"

"No. When Alexander the Great captured Babylon in 331 BCE, he wanted to repair it, but eventually decided to simply demolish it and start over. He died before the new tower could be built. The ruins are still there, though."

Aliyah, who had been listening intently, now snapped at Kismet. "The elemental? Did you see it?"

"I did, but…" Kismet's forehead creased in a frown. "I'm not exactly sure what it was. At first, it was a sword. Single edge, with a curve. Like a machete."

"A *kopis*." Aliyah's voice was an eager whisper.

"What you saw was the sword of Alexander the Great, which he used to cut apart the Gordian Knot."

Maddock knew that story well. According to legend, in the city of Gordium in Phrygia—modern-day Turkey—there was an ox-cart tied to a post with an impossibly complicated knot. Alexander's oracle told him that if he could untie the knot, he would rule all of Asia, but when his attempts to do so by conventional means failed, he took a more direct approach, slicing the knot apart with his sword.

"That makes sense," Maddock said, thinking aloud. "The fourth tarot suit is swords. Maybe Alexander got the sword from the temple in Babylon and used it to cut the knot."

"The timing isn't quite right though," Rose countered. "The incident with the Gordian Knot happened in 333 BCE. That was before he conquered Babylon."

Kismet raised a hand. "There's more. It was a sword, but then it was something else. A piece of something that looked like green glass. Flat like a slab. There were marks on it. Some kind of writing, but I didn't recognize it."

Aliyah's eyes widened and she turned to Black, sharing a look of mutual disbelief. She mouthed something and he nodded. "Could it have been emerald?" she asked aloud.

Kismet nodded. "Yes. Why? Do you know what it is?"

She regarded him with a look that was, at once,

both contemplative and contemptuous. "I believe it is the Tabula Smaragdina. The Emerald Tablet."

Maddock looked to Rose then Jade but neither showed any sign of recognition.

"I've heard of that," Kismet said. "It's an alchemical manuscript, isn't it?"

"It is the original alchemical manuscript," Aliyah said. "The revelation of Hermes Trismegistus, who is also called Thoth of Egypt, carved on a tablet of indestructible emerald. It is the basis for the Hermetic tradition. The tablet was discovered and translated in the 8th Century by Balinas in the city of Tyana in Cappadocia. Like the books of the Bible, the text of the Tabula Smaragdina has been reproduced many times, but the whereabouts of the original tablet are unknown.

"Perhaps the Emerald Tablet was there, in Babel, in the Etemenanki, in the time of Alexander the Great. Perhaps that is the symbolism of the story of the Gordian Knot; knowledge as sharp as a blade. Or perhaps the tablet, like the Magna of Illusion, is itself a talisman of great power." She continued to stare at Kismet, some of her anger giving way to cool calculation. "We are meant to have it. And I believe you are meant to find it."

"So you're taking my advice?" Kismet replied evenly. "Giving up on revenge?"

Aliyah's smile was as sharp and cold as a blade. "Your friends will remain here, as a guarantee of your good conduct. They will be well cared for, provided you continue to cooperate." She conspicuously dodged his question. "Together we will find the pyramid in the ice, and when we have the third element, we will use all three to find the Emerald Tablet."

Kismet held her stare, but Maddock saw a change in the man's eyes; an unspoken message to him. *Get ready.*

"I told you what I saw." Kismet spoke slowly, his tone calm, measured, but hard as diamond. "You promised to let them go."

"And I will," Aliyah retorted. "In due time."

"That wasn't the deal. You swore an oath."

Aliyah's smile faltered, the accusation clearly troubling to her if only because she had an audience.

"But that's okay," Kismet said, smiling, "because I haven't been completely honest with you. Now!"

Kismet moved so quickly that, even though Maddock was expecting it, he was taken completely by surprise. Kismet sprang at Aliyah like a rattlesnake striking, but he did not attack her. Instead, he raked his hand across hers, stripping the Apex from her grip. As he closed his fist around the talisman, he pivoted away from her, racing instead toward Rose, arms thrown wide as if he intended to tackle her.

Which was exactly what he did.

The fraction of a second it took for him to do all of this was roughly equal to Maddock's reaction time, but he hesitated a moment longer, unsure of where to focus his attention. Jade, with a pistol still pressed against her throat, was in the most immediate danger, but trying to wrest the gun from the hands of her captor was a monumentally bad idea. And the situation wasn't much better for the rest of them. He figured he had maybe another fraction of a second—the time it would take to blink—before the shooting started.

Why did he go to Rose?

The thought barely had time to flit through his brain before the answer arrived in spectacular fashion. From one moment to the next, everything changed. The gunmen adjusted their aim, fingers tightening on triggers, and then—

blink

—they were swept off their feet, hurled backward and slammed into the perimeter walls. It was as if an enormous balloon had instantaneously inflated, like a car's airbag following a collision, filling the room with its bulk, pushing the gunmen away and pinning them against the walls. Most were still gripping their pistols and flashlights, but the hands that held them were immobilized by the invisible force. Aliyah and Black had been caught up as well. Entangled like lovers, they were plastered against the rear wall near the vault door. Yet, the heavy door was still open, undisturbed by the effect. Maddock had felt nothing. Bones and Jade were likewise untouched, gaping in disbelief as they attempted to process what had just happened.

Rose was still on the ground, with Kismet covering her, hugging her… No, it wasn't an embrace. He was reaching around her, his hands pressed against the orb in her backpack.

The orb.

Maddock recalled how, in the Antarctic Outpost, the Prometheus strike team leader had used the orb to create an impenetrable bubble of energy, a force-field that protected him from bullets. Rose had tried to use it to do the same during their subsequent escape. They had survived unscathed though whether that had anything to do with the orb or Rose's ability to master it, Maddock could not say. But Kismet *had* succeeded in tapping into the orb's power, using it together with the Apex, to melt the ice away from Grace's frozen cadaver, and now it seemed he had done it again.

Kismet bounded to his feet and then reached out a hand to help Rose stand, but in that instant, the effect began to wane. Maddock saw Aliyah peel one arm away from the wall, using it to brace herself and push her entire body away. Her henchmen were similarly breaking free of the rapidly diminishing force.

Kismet looked to Maddock. "The mirror."

Maddock did a quick visual sweep, locating the box containing the Magna of Illusion. It had fallen from Black's grasp and now lay in the center of the room. He darted forward and picked it up, verifying that the flawless obsidian disk was still inside. "Got it!"

"Then let's get the hell out of here!"

17

"**I'll just ask** the obvious question," Bones said as they hurried down the path at a near-jog, as fast as they dared move in the darkness. "Why are we in such a hurry? We've got all three magic doodads, and you obviously know how to use them. They mess with us again, just put the whammy on 'em."

Without breaking stride, Kismet looked back over his shoulder. "You ever see Wizard of Oz?"

"Who hasn't?"

"You remember how Dorothy killed the witches?"

Bones shrugged. "Sure. She dropped a house on one, and melted the other with a bucket of water."

"She got lucky. Twice. I got lucky back there. I caught them by surprise. But they know a lot more about these things than I do, and maybe I won't get lucky a second time."

Maddock thought about his answer, remembering how Aliyah had tried to use the Apex and the Magna of Illusion together—tried and failed. Kismet was wrong, he decided. When it came to tapping the power of the elementals, the magicians were as much in the dark as everyone else.

Still, probably best not to put all their eggs in that basket.

They descended the moss-slick stairs and hurried out onto the pier. The rain was coming down harder now, the seas noticeably rougher. Storm waves, rebounding off the headlands and coming in from every conceivable direction, were pounding the cliffs and throwing curtains of spray over the pier. When they reached the steps leading down to the dock, Maddock half-expected to find their boat gone, torn from its mooring, but instead there were now three Zodiacs tied to the cleats. Both the dock and the inflatable boats were rising and falling a good three feet with each swell that rolled through.

By mutual accord, Maddock and Bones hurried ahead to the nearest boat, steadying it, at least to the extent that was possible, so the others could board. Rose climbed in first and as soon as she was seated, Maddock passed the box with the Magna of Illusion over to her. She accepted it without comment, slipping it into the pack with the orb. Jade boarded next but Kismet moved past them, to the next Zodiac.

"What? You too good to ride with us?" Bones called out.

Kismet laughed. "I'm not going to ride in it."

His hand dropped to his waist and, with a noise like fingernails on a chalkboard, he drew an enormous *kukri* knife from a concealed sheath and slashed it across the bright yellow inflatable gunwale. Air rushed from the ruptured cell in a flatulent whoosh. The boat did not immediately sink, but as the buoyancy chamber emptied, the craft settled lower, and water began sloshing over the gunwale, filling the bilges.

"It leaks."

He did the same to the other boat then sheathed his knife and rejoined the others, clambering into the Zodiac with Rose and Jade. Maddock went next, immediately settling into the pilot's chair, while Bones loosened but did not release the knot around the cleat. With the raft still rising and falling crazily with the sea, their timing would have to be perfect. Cast off at the wrong moment, and they might get thrown against the pier.

After checking to make sure the shift lever was in the neutral position, Maddock hit the electric starter switch, revved the motor once, twice, and then looked out to sea, watching the swells roll in. The Zodiac dipped as one wave passed, and then just as quickly began rising with the next. When it reached the crest, Maddock shouted, "Now!"

Bones gave the rope a deft twist and then leaped into the prow. His momentum caused the front end to swing away from the dock, and as the boat tilted toward the backside of the wave, it fell away from the mooring, sliding faster down the wave. At the same instant, Maddock engaged the screws and opened up the throttle. The Zodiac shot forward but almost immediately began to nose up, into the next swell.

"Hang on!"

The boat angled up, climbing the fluid slope,

but as it neared the crest, he eased off the throttle to avoid shooting off the top like a rocket. Their momentum carried them over the hump and then they were falling again.

This roller coaster ride replayed again and again as they fought clear of Drake's Island. The rain continued to lash them, but as they reached the deeper water in the channel, the ride finally smoothed out a little, so Maddock gave it more throttle and pointed the bow toward Plymouth harbor. The city lights appeared to undulate up and down as the Zodiac skipped over rough seas, a tapestry of stars waving up and down as if being shaken by a giant.

But two of the lights were different. Low on the horizon, they didn't move the same as the others. More precisely, they *were* moving, detached from the fixed cityscape which only seemed to be in motion.

Two boats, exiting the harbor, heading out into the storm-tossed sound.

Probably nothing. A couple of fisherman taking their boats out to deep water to avoid the incessant pounding of the storm surge.

But Maddock's instincts told him otherwise.

He cut back on the throttle, which eased the relentless hammering vibrations from the hull smashing through the waves, but perversely made the nausea-inducing rise and fall even more pronounced.

Bones crawled back to him. "You saw 'em, too?"

Maddock nodded. He resisted the urge to dismiss what he had seen, what he was feeling. If it was nothing, it was nothing, but if it wasn't nothing, denial would only make the situation worse.

"You think witchy-poo had some reinforcements standing by?"

"Could be."

Kismet joined them. "There's another possibility."

"Prometheus."

"They might have been hanging back, waiting for us to do the heavy lifting."

"Bastards," Bones snarled.

"Typical," Kismet said, affirming the sentiment.

Maddock nodded. "So how do we—down!"

Tiny flashes of light, barely visible beside the brighter spotlights of the approaching vessels, eliminated the first possibility.

Definitely not nothing.

18

Bullets whizzed overhead with a hiss that was audible, even over the tumult of the storm and the roar of the outboard. Multiple reports, the distinctive crack of supersonic rifle rounds.

"Anyone planning to do something about that?" Bones said. "You know, like maybe raise shields?"

Rose shrugged off the backpack and shoved it toward Kismet. "You're the expert."

Kismet shook his head, more a gesture of resignation than uncertainty and reached for it, but before he could take it, Rose snatched it back. "Crap! I forgot."

"What?"

"We can't use shields."

Another volley split the air overhead, and then something thumped against one of the gunwales. Air erupted from a ragged hole in the buoyancy tube.

Bones scrambled forward and slapped one massive hand over the leak. "Check the lockers. Should be a repair kit in one of them."

"Idiots," Jade raged as she crawled forward to check the bow locker. "If they sink us, they'll lose the elementals."

"If it's Prometheus," Kismet countered, "they won't care. They have the resources to recover them."

Determining the exact identity of their attackers was a secondary priority for Maddock. Every passing second was bringing them closer to the shooters.

He cranked the wheel, cutting hard to port, carving a tight 180° turn. The lights of Plymouth were swept away, replaced by the scattered lights of rural Cornwall. In the distance, perhaps two miles away, lay a single shining beacon, the Plymouth Breakwater Lighthouse, marking the west end of the nearly mile-long manmade barrier that guarded the entrance to the bay. Maddock pointed the bow toward it and opened up the throttle.

He glanced over at Rose, who was now hugging the backpack to her chest protectively. "Rose, why can't we use the orb?"

"I just remembered something from the Dodge Dalton books. The shield is some kind of electrical field. If it comes into contact with water—"

Maddock understood. "We're toast."

"Pretty much."

Bones glanced over his shoulder and shook his head. "What's the point of having magic gizmos if they never work when you need them to."

"I don't think it's real magic," Rose said. "Just a technology we don't understand."

"Well it's pretty freaking useless either way."

"Will a first aid kit work?" Jade asked, holding up a white plastic box embossed with a big red cross.

"Is there tape in it?"

Jade popped the case open and held up a fat white donut-shaped roll of adhesive cloth. "Will this do?"

Bones shrugged and reached out with his free hand to take it.

The dark, unlit mass of Drake's Island hove into view directly ahead. *Right back where we started,* Maddock thought as he veered away from the peer angling left to hug the eastern edge of the island. As it slid by, he wondered if Aliyah and her minions were watching from the shadowy cliffs.

A glance back showed the light of the two boats hunting them, maybe two hundred yards back, matching their pace. They were easily within rifle range, and while the turbulent seas would challenge even an experienced shooter, fickle Lady Luck could easily turn her back on them.

His intent was to follow the curve of the island toward the south shore, putting the landmass between them and the hunters, but the increasingly rough seas forced him to abandon that idea. The only way to survive the incoming waves was by taking them head on.

And how long can I keep that up? he wondered.

Bones uttered a harsh curse and flung the roll of white first aid tape out into the sea. Maddock didn't need to ask what the problem was; the surface of the buoyancy tube was too wet for the tape to adhere. The inflatable boat wouldn't sink, not right away, but as the tube continued to deflate, the hull would ride lower and the sea would find its way in.

"Not long enough," he muttered. It was time for a new plan. And a new boat.

19

With a sickening crunch, the Zodiac's rigid hull rode up onto the Plymouth Breakwater and shuddered to a halt. Even though she had braced herself for the expected impact, Jade was nearly catapulted over the increasingly flaccid buoyancy tube. She waited for the rebound, and then did the very thing the collision had failed to accomplish.

She landed badly, the rocks beneath her were slippery and uneven, but in the fraction of a second it took for her to fall face-first into them, a roiling wave rushed in, covering the surface. The suddenly knee-deep water didn't cushion her fall so much as prolong it, dragging her another six feet up onto the sloping artificial reef, pummeling and scraping her body even as the sea water rushed over her head, blinding her, nearly choking her.

"Great plan, Maddock!" she snarled.

Despite the sarcastic tone of her observation, she knew it was probably the best plan given their dire circumstance. With the pair of hunters pushing them further into the teeth of the storm, and a boat that wouldn't be seaworthy much longer, getting out of the water was imperative.

She struggled to hands and knees, the rough stone abrading her skin, but it was enough to get her head clear. The wave's energy abruptly reversed, pulling her back, threatening to carry her out to sea, but she spread-eagled on the slick rock, anchoring herself until the sucking sensation passed.

Through the blurry haze, she could just make out the dark silhouette of the breakwater, and beyond it, the night sky, briefly illuminated in the glow of a signal flash from the lighthouse.

That was where she needed to go, but Maddock's plan required one thing of her first. She turned her head searching the surf, but the light was already fading, plunging her into near total darkness. "Rose!"

"Here!" The answering voice was weak, more a sputtering cough than a shout, but a moment later, Jade felt something tugging at the hem of her shirt. She groped to find Rose's hand and took it in her grip as another wave surged in and drove them both further up onto the breakwater. Jade clung to both the rocks under her, and to Rose's outstretched hand until the wave retreated. Another bright flash from the lighthouse lit up the sky above, and indirectly, the route they would need to take to reach the elevated crest of the breakwater. It also revealed Nick Kismet, clinging to Rose's other hand.

The crest of the mile-long breakwater was a flat paved platform, about forty feet wide, and mostly above the pounding surf. Working together, the trio made it to the top, just as the signal light flashed yet again. Jade glanced back. There was no sign of Maddock or Bones, but she easily spotted the two boats, closing in on the breakwater, just a few hundred yards out. She shook her head and focused on her own survival.

Kismet urged them forward at a run. Maddock had grounded the Zodiac about a hundred yards east of the lighthouse. Not far, but up on the crest of the breakwater, they would be silhouetted against the sky, easy targets for the killers in the boats. The only thing going for them was the fact that the men would not have a stable platform from which to take that shot. She didn't hear any reports—though they might have easily been drowned out by the pounding surf—and hoped that meant the shooters had reached the same conclusion. Even so, taking cover behind the lighthouse was the number one priority.

The base of the Plymouth Breakwater lighthouse was flared like the pedestal of a floor lamp, nearly twice as wide as at the top. The entrance faced more or less in the direction from which they had just come, but it would almost certainly be locked up tight, and even if they somehow were able to get it open, being inside the automated signaling station would give them no advantage. Just the opposite, they would be cornered, with no exit. Instead, they bypassed the door and veered to the left, circling around it clockwise until the great bulk of the lighthouse was between them and the men with guns. Kismet stopped, delved into Rose's backpack—which he had been carrying since they hatched the crazy plan—and brought out the orb, while Jade and Rose moved along the base in opposite directions to keep an eye on their pursuers.

They didn't have to wait long.

From her vantage on the south side of the lighthouse, Jade could see them moving along the breakwater. She reckoned there were five or six of them, though it was hard to tell as they were bunched up and obscured by rain and shadow. As they drew closer, they split into two groups heading different directions around the light. Jade backed away and hurried back to join Kismet. Rose had arrived a few seconds ahead of her and had already given Kismet the news.

"You two better take cover," Kismet said, hugging the orb to his chest. "If this doesn't work… Hell, even if it does, you're not going to want to be anywhere close to me."

"If it doesn't work," Jade replied, "You should throw that thing into the sea."

"Let me just go on record one more time," Rose put in. "This is a really terrible idea. You're going to get yourself killed."

"Don't worry about me." He nodded in the direction of the squat concrete cube-shaped structure that stood halfway between the light and the water's edge. "Go. Now."

Jade had no idea what purpose the stout structure served but it looked bulletproof. She and Rose hastened behind the building, but Jade immediately peeked around the corner to watch the confrontation.

She heard shouts, one of the gunmen ordering Kismet to put his hands up. Kismet didn't answer, didn't move.

"Come on," Jade whispered, and then remembering Bones' earlier comment, added. "Show 'em the whammy!"

For a few seconds, nothing happened. Then, everything happened all at once.

The air around Kismet lit up with the brilliance of an arc welder, accompanied by the deafening *crack* of an electrical discharge. Jade closed her eyes and drew back, but the damage was already done. The sight of Kismet—just his silhouette really—surrounded by long tendrils of lighting, was burned into her eyes like a snapshot. The afterimage dissolved into the green blob of temporary flash blindness, but she didn't need her eyes to follow what was happening on the other side of the concrete structure.

The crackle and pop of voltage, the distinctive smell of ozone in the air. Other sounds and smells joined the tumult. The reports of a rifle, several of them. The sulfur stink of burnt gunpowder.

Kismet!

Then she felt something, like invisible cobwebs brushing against her face, an uncomfortable tingling sensation that crept all over her body.

"Rose! Get down!"

Jade barely had time to follow her own advice before lightning struck. That was what it felt like. The flash from the other side of the concrete cube was so bright that even through the green spots in her vision, the world was lit up like daybreak. The subsequent thunderclap shook the ground and drove the breath from her lungs.

And then, silence.

20

After intentionally running the Zodiac aground on the breakwater, Maddock and Bones had also gone into the water, but unlike Jade and the others, they had stayed there, watching and waiting.

And waiting.

The plan was simple. Divide and conquer, though in this instance, they would be the ones dividing their forces. Kismet, Jade and Rose would go ashore and hopefully draw most of the killers after them, and—again hopefully—unleash the orb's power to defeat the gunmen. While the three of them were doing that, Maddock and Bones would lie low—literally—staying partially submerged in the surf, hiding under the wreckage of the Zodiac until the boats came in. Once the gunmen took the bait, the two of them would sneak aboard one or both of the boats, overpower whatever crew remained, after which they would regroup and head back to Plymouth, leaving their would-be attackers stranded on the breakwater.

Simple. And far from perfect.

The abandoned Zodiac to which Maddock and Bones clung was just so much flotsam, alternately slammed into the breakwater by the storm waves and then dragged back out into the sea. The water was a hypothermia-inducing 50° Fahrenheit, but he and Bones had trained under harsher conditions in the course of their SEAL training, and knew their limitations. Maddock figured they could last at least half an hour if they had to, maybe longer. It wouldn't be pleasant. In fact, between the pummeling, the cold, and having to listen to Bones whine about "shrinkage," it would be absolute hell.

Kismet and the others would face a different set of problems. He had already twice proven his ability to control the otherworldly talisman, and Maddock felt certain their new friend would be able to deliver once again, but there was no telling what would happen when he attempted to use the orb to create an electrical force field in the rain. There was a very real chance that the orb would short out, leaving them defenseless, or even electrocute Kismet, but he had assured them all that he could handle whatever happened.

The real problem with the plan was that everything depended on the bad guys doing exactly what Maddock wanted them to do. If they didn't take the bait, come ashore on the breakwater and chase after Kismet and the others, it would all be for nothing.

Yet, what choice did they have? The Zodiac wouldn't have lasted much longer. Better to abandon it with solid ground underfoot. Worst case scenario, it would be a stalemate, and that was better than drowning in the English Channel.

They didn't have to wait long. The boats—gray and black RIBs, military versions of the Zodiac— came in cautiously, running the screws in reverse, then forward, to hold station about twenty yards off the rocks. Maddock counted eight men—four in each boat—all wearing tactical black from head-to-toe. Either Aliyah's magicians had a special operations division, which he doubted, or these guys were working for Prometheus.

One by one, three men from each boat fearlessly took the plunge. They vanished into the water, reappearing a few seconds later in the frothy surf. They scuttled up onto the rocks, moving on all fours like crabs. The two pilots shone their spotlights onto the shoreline until all six men were accounted for, then revved their motors, backing the boats away from the breakwater, getting clear of the surf.

"If we're going to do this," Bones started.

"I know," Maddock said, fighting to keep his teeth from chattering. "I've got right. You take left."

"Sure," Bones growled. "Make me swim further."

The big man ducked his head under the surface and was gone before Maddock could point out that there was no meaningful difference in the distance to the two RIBs, respectively. Maddock shook his head, fixed the location of the boat in his mind, and then after drawing in a deep breath, submerged himself and started swimming underwater.

His sodden clothes reduced his natural buoyancy to the point where he barely had to exert himself to stay submerged, and since he could hold his breath for well over two minutes, there was no need to come to the surface until he was right where he wanted to be. There really wasn't much risk of being seen by the pilots of the two boats, not unless they happened to move their lights to shine them directly on the spot where he was going to break the surface, but Maddock was a believer in Murphy's Law—if something can go wrong, it will—and he planned accordingly. Years of real-world experience gave him an almost supernatural sense of where he was in relation to the other boat, but he allowed a generous margin of error just in case.

When he was fairly certain of his position, he allowed himself to drift back up to the surface. As soon as his head cleared the water, he spotted the silhouette of the nearest RIB, about fifteen meters away, and right between him and the breakwater.

Perfect.

He repositioned to face the vessel's stern and began pulling himself through the water using a slow breast stroke that kept just his eyes and nose above the waterline. At first, he could only make out the outline of the man sitting in the pilot's chair but as he got closer and the angle of his line of sight became sharper, the man disappeared behind the bulk of the outboard. Fortunately, that would work both ways; the man in the boat would not see him coming either.

He dog-paddled closer, one hand outstretched and resting against the engine cowling to maintain a safe distance from the boat until he was ready to make his move. The outboard was still running at idle but that could change at any moment and with no warning at all. The last thing Maddock needed was for a swell to throw him into the screws just as they began turning. Carefully, so as not to transmit any vibrations through the hull, he pulled himself in close, grasping the molded stern just to the right of the engine cowling, and then slowly, stealthily, pulled himself up onto the molded transom and—

Froze as he realized he was looking down the barrel of a gun.

Crap! Maddock thought. As careful as he had been, somehow the man had sensed his presence. *So much for the stealthy approach. I hope Bones is having better luck.*

The muzzle was just a couple inches from his face, close enough that even in the low light conditions, he could tell that it was bored for a 5.56-millimeter round—an AR-15 variant of some kind. Definitely not the same kind of hardware Aliyah's magick order had been packing. The weapon was close enough that, under any other circumstances, he would have been tempted to grab the barrel, redirect it away from his face and yank it out of the gunman's hands, but his precarious position on the stern of the RIB made that a risky proposition. Not out of the question, but risky enough that he decided to consider other options.

He raised his eyes, looking past the barrel to the face of the man who held the weapon. The man was grinning, a big, hungry grin that made Maddock think of the Big Bad Wolf from Little Red Riding

Hood.

My what big teeth you have....

"Dane Maddock," the grinning man exclaimed, as if they were long-lost friends. "Well, I'd be lying if I said it was a surprise to see you. TBH, I would have been disappointed if you hadn't tried something like this."

A chill that had nothing to do with the water temperature shot through Maddock. He didn't recognize the grinning man's face, but there was no mistaking the voice. Or his bizarre insistence on using "text-ese" abbreviations in everyday speech.

TBH.

That was the name he had given to the faceless leader of the Prometheus strike team that tried to capture the orb in the Outpost in Antarctica.

"No," he gasped. "No way. You're dead!"

Maddock was certain of that. TBH had been impaled on the adamantine-infused blade of the tomahawk that had led them to the orb and awakened its power. The hatchet head had gone clean through his chest. It was a mortal injury. Unsurvivable even under the best of circumstances with immediate medical attention.

TBH grinned again. "It didn't take."

A swell rocked the boat under them and water sloshed over Maddock's head but the weapon aimed at him did not waver.

"How?"

TBH laughed. "Ask my brother. Oh, wait. I

guess you're not going to get a chance to do that." He paused a second and then added, "You know, because you'll be dead."

Maddock barely registered the threat—

Brother?

—but at the other end of the rifle, the Prometheus leader squared his shoulders and curled his finger around the trigger.

21

A flash, not of superheated gas driving a bullet down the barrel of the rifle and into Maddock's face, but of a lightning bolt striking somewhere just past the lighthouse on the breakwater, lit up the world. TBH's eyes shifted to the side, his attention diverted just for an instant.

Maddock was similarly distracted by the flash, but knew better than to let this momentary reprieve slip away. He put all thought of his foe's seemingly miraculous recovery out of his head, along with the man's cryptic pronouncement—*ask my brother*— and jerked his head to the side, just enough to removed himself from the direct line of fire. In the same motion, he reached up with his right hand to grasp the barrel, shoving it in the opposite direction.

The metal was suddenly hot in his grip and he felt the concussive force of an impact slam into his palm as the weapon discharged, sending a 5.56 round sizzling harmlessly past him, into the sea. Maddock felt like his hand had been slapped with Thor's hammer, but he did not let go of the barrel. Instead, he twisted his body sideways, pulling the rifle toward him. TBH, with his hand still curled around the pistol grip did not let go either, and because he had nothing to brace himself against, toppled forward, over the transom and into the water.

Maddock, still hanging onto the rifle, let go of

the boat and threw his left arm around the Prometheus leader in a hug that pinned the man's arms to his side, even as both of them plunged beneath the surface. Maddock felt the other man's struggles growing more frantic and squeezed even tighter.

Weighed down by his heavy tactical gear, spare magazines and the seven-pound rifle, TBH sank like a stone, taking Maddock with him. As they descended, Maddock began counting the seconds. He could gauge their depth by the growing pressure against his eardrums. At ten feet, it was merely uncomfortable. At twenty it was actually painful. He began working his jaw and blowing through his nose to pop his ears and equalize the pressure. That brought only a few seconds of comfort, a few more vertical feet of descent.

Ten Mississippi... Eleven Mississippi....

TBH was thrashing now, desperately trying to squirm free, but Maddock did not let go. Abruptly, the descent stopped. With all the squirming, Maddock had not even felt the soft touch of the seafloor beneath him.

Sometime after his fortieth Mississippi, TBH's spasms became even more violent. He went as rigid as a flagpole, and then stopped moving completely. Maddock's own lungs were starting to burn with the need to breathe, but he held on a little longer just to be sure. He was pretty sure the man was dead, but he had thought that after their encounter at the

Outpost as well.

You're dead... It didn't take... Ask my brother.

My brother.

When he got to sixty, Maddock disentangled, shoved the unmoving form of his would-be killer away, and began swimming for the surface. He hoped Bones had been luckier than he, hoped also that Jade, Rose and Kismet had survived their encounter with the rest of the Prometheus strike team. The strange electrical discharge might have just been a lightning strike, but Maddock's gut told him it was nothing so mundane.

The climb back to the surface took another thirty seconds, taxing the limits of even Maddock's extraordinary lung capacity, and by the time he finally broke through, the only thing he cared about was breathing fresh air. He gasped in several breaths, coughing out the seawater that had insinuated itself into his mouth and nose, and began searching for the RIB.

A light flashed in his eyes. He blinked and looked away, just as something struck him in the head. The blow wasn't hard enough to cause real pain; it felt almost like a jab from someone wearing boxing gloves. A moment later, he felt the object bump into him again, and realized what it was: A ring-shaped foam life preserver.

"You going to grab that?" Bones called out to him. "Just pretend it's your junk, because I'm not coming in after you."

22

Maddock grinned as the light moved away from him. He threaded one arm through the ring and hugged it to his chest as Bones began reeling him in. He could just make out the outline of the RIB, maybe twenty feet away, and his friend hauling him in like a prize catch.

"Always gotta do things the hard way," said Bones as he leaned out and pulled Maddock up and over the gunwale.

"Believe me, it wasn't by choice." Maddock decided not to share the news about the identity of the man he had just fought with. That could wait until later. "Any sign of the others?"

"Not really. Just that big flash and then nothing. Did you see it?"

Maddock nodded but did not articulate his fears about what it signified. He struggled to a sitting position. "Get me ashore. I'll go check it out."

"Thought you might want to do that. Here. I found this—well, inherited it would be more accurate. Might come in handy." Bones passed over an assault weapon—an M4 carbine if Maddock was not mistaken—and then turned to take his place at the console. The RIB lurched as Bones engaged the screws and a few seconds later, Maddock was in the water again, splashing up onto the storm barrier.

Once he was above the surf, he brought the carbine to the low ready and made his way up the sloping breakwater. He paused just below the crest, scanning the path before him for any sign of activity, hostile or otherwise. Every few seconds, a flash from the lighthouse obliquely illumed the foreground but aside from the crashing sea and the persistent rain splattering on the paving stones, all was still.

He brought the weapon up, staring through its attached EOTech holographic sight, finger poised alongside the trigger, and started toward the towering structure. He moved quickly, with short strides, rolling his feet heel-to-toe to maintain traction and avoid stumbling over unseen obstacles, and reached the base of the lighthouse in less than a minute. He turned left, intending to make a clockwise circle, but after only a few degrees of the arc, he heard something over the din of the storm.

Jade's voice. She was counting. And cursing.

"Five… Six… Seven… Eight… Breathe, damn it."

Maddock hastened in the direction of the sound, lowering the weapon, but remaining poised to revert to a more aggressive stance at the first sign of danger.

There was no need however. As he came around to the south side of the tower, he spotted them in the intermittent flash of the beacon. Rose stood by helplessly as a kneeling Jade pumped Kismet's chest with her crossed hands, and counted and cursed. When she reached fifteen, she bent over and breathed into his mouth.

The orb lay a few feet away from them, looking about as deadly as a concrete lawn ornament.

Maddock ran to them, shouting. "What happened?"

Rose started at the sound of his approach, but then fell into his arms, openly weeping. "The rain. When he tried to use it..." She faltered, words failing her, but Maddock had already figured it out. As Rose had feared, Kismet's attempt to use the orb to create an electrical force field had backfired. Evidently, it had not been a complete failure. The Prometheus gunmen had been swept away, probably blasted into the ocean, but Kismet had paid the ultimate price for that victory. The current had ripped through him, blasting him like an actual bolt of lightning, stopping his heart.

Maddock shook himself into action. Jade had done the right thing in starting CPR, but that alone wouldn't save Kismet's life. Despite what happened in movies, chest compressions could not start a stopped heart. Even the ubiquitous flatline on the EKG monitor was a complete fiction; the heart beat its life-sustaining rhythm because of electrical impulses from the brain, impulses that continued in some form even after death. The EKG was a representation of the electrical signals that kept the heart beating, not the actual activity of the heart muscle. Cardio-pulmonary resuscitation primarily served to forestall brain death by sustaining the flow of oxygenated blood to the brain and organs, but the only way to restore the heart's normal rhythm was with a jolt from a defibrillator, and the nearest one of those was back in Plymouth harbor.

He turned to Rose. "The orb did this, right? Maybe we can use it to jump start his heart again."

Rose gaped at him, horrified. "And end up just like him?"

Maddock wasn't so sure. Kismet had some kind of affinity for the orb and the other elemental artifacts, an affinity nobody else seemed to have. Except for TBH, of course.

Ask my brother….

Maddock didn't know how to put that into words, so he chose instead to simply act. He stepped forward and, bracing himself for the possibility that he was about to make a fatal mistake, scooped up the orb

Nothing. Not even a tingle of current.

"So far, so good." He turned, faced Jade and Kismet. "Get clear," he warned.

Jade looked up, her lips moving as she continued counting, and shook her head.

Rose ran forward, putting herself in between him and the others. "Maddock, don't."

Maddock was about to attempt an explanation, but just then, Kismet's entire body spasmed, like someone waking from a dream of falling, and he gasped loudly.

Jade backpedaled away, as if uncertain whether this was a miraculous recovery, or some kind of zombie-like reanimation. Maddock was similarly wary, but Kismet merely sat up, looking bewildered. He met Maddock's gaze and raised a hopeful eyebrow. "Did it work?"

You were dead... It didn't take... Ask my brother.

Maddock extended a hand and helped Kismet to his feet. The latter bounded up, as if his near-death experience was nothing but a refreshing nap. Maddock maintained the handclasp pulling Kismet even closer.

"I ran into your brother," he said, his voice low, almost a whisper. "We need to talk."

EPILOGUE—The Final Element

During the train ride back to London that night, Kismet told them the whole story, beginning with his first encounter with Prometheus and the man he now knew to be his estranged brother. The first glimpse behind what he called "the shroud of heaven" had set him on a path of discovery—not only about the true nature of reality and spirituality, but also of a mystery that began the day of his own birth.

He revealed that his father, Christian Garral, was not his true biological father. The man had adopted him shortly after his birth and subsequent abandonment. He had known that much even as a young boy, but it was only much later that he learned the unusual circumstances of his birth and parentage. Adam Garral was not, so far as Kismet knew, a blood relative.

The man Maddock called TBH, and who had identified himself to Kismet as Ulrich Hauser, was actually Kismet's fraternal twin, and while Kismet had grown up as the son of a globe-trotting adventurer and yacht racer, his brother had been groomed to lead Prometheus, an education overseen by the mother Kismet had never met.

"Your contact on the inside," Maddock realized aloud.

Kismet just nodded.

It was not merely inevitable that the two men

would cross paths again, but foreordained.

Kismet also told them of his other adventures, such as his descent into the Black Sea to find the Golden Fleece of Greek legend, or his battle against a diabolical monk to control the Judas rope.

"Wait," Bones interrupted. "Judas, as in Jesus's bro?"

Kismet nodded. "According to the story, it was the rope Judas Iscariot used to hang himself with after the betrayal. I don't know if it's true, but sometimes it's easier just to go with the devil you know."

Bones and Maddock exchanged knowing looks, but kept their silence.

Kismet's final confrontation with his brother—though now it seemed not-quite-so-final after all—had involved a search for the secret of immortality itself. Though he had been a skeptic at the outset, subsequent events had made him a believer.

Bones shook his head in disbelief. "You're immortal?"

"I honestly don't know," replied Kismet. "The effects may wear off someday, but right now… Yeah, I guess 'immortal' sums it up. I look about twenty years younger than what is says on my driver's license."

"If I ever settle down with a hot, young number, maybe you can give her a bit of what you've got," Bones said.

"You'll be settling down with your left hand," Jade said.

"I heal quickly," Kismet went on. Even from very serious injuries." He nodded in Jade's direction. "And if I don't get a haircut at least once a week, or I start looking like Cousin It."

Bones wagged his head again. "Kismet, means luck, right?"

"Luck. Fate. Serendipity. Take your pick."

"Well, I think you must be the luckiest son-of-a-bitch on the planet."

"Fortune favors the bold," said Jade.

Kismet gave a mirthless chuckle. "Believe me, I don't feel particularly lucky."

"And your brother got a dose of it, too?" said Maddock.

Kismet shrugged. "I didn't think so at the time, but based on what you've told me, that's about the only conclusion I can draw."

"So he's just going to keep coming?" Bones said. "Like Arnie?" He dropped his voice and affected a comically thick Austrian accent. "I'll be bah-ck."

"Until he gets what he wants. The Philosopher's Stone."

"So we get it first, yeah?" said Jade. "Use it against him. If it can give immortality, maybe it can take it away, too." A guilty look came over her and she quickly glanced over at Kismet. "We'd be careful with it, of course."

Maddock looked over at Rose, who held the backpack containing the orb and mirror on her lap. "First we have to find the fourth elemental. The

Emerald Tablet."

Kismet stared at Maddock. "You don't have to, you know. This is my fight. And, not to put too fine a point on it, but I've got nine lives. You don't."

Bones laughed. "Not to put too fine a point on it, but you'd be nowhere without us. Stopping bad guys from taking over the world is kind of our thing."

Kismet glanced at him and then the others. "Does he speak for all of you?"

Jade gave a derisive snort and shook her head. "God forbid. But I was on board before he showed up, so I've already got dibs."

"I don't want to think about what will happen if Prometheus wins this fight," said Maddock, "but I know we'll stand a better chance if we stick together."

Kismet nodded slowly. "All right. Then let's do this."

The End

If you enjoyed *Arcanum*, don't miss *Magus*, the final book of the *Elementals* trilogy!

ABOUT THE AUTHORS

David Wood is the USA Today bestselling author of the action-adventure series, The Dane Maddock Adventures, and many other works. He also writes fantasy under his David Debord pen name. When not writing, he hosts the Wood on Words podcast. David and his family live in Santa Fe, New Mexico. Visit him online at davidwoodweb.com.

Sean Ellis has authored and co-authored more than two dozen action-adventure novels, including the Nick Kismet adventures, the Jack Sigler/Chess Team series with Jeremy Robinson, and the Jade Ihara adventures with David Wood. He served with the Army National Guard in Afghanistan, and has a Bachelor of Science degree in Natural Resources Policy from Oregon State University. Sean is also a member of the International Thriller Writers organization. He currently resides in Arizona, where he divides his time between writing, adventure sports, and trying to figure out how to save the world. Learn more about Sean at seanellisauthor.com

.

Made in the USA
Middletown, DE
19 July 2019